FATED MATE DADDY BEAR

BRIDGE HOLLOW SHIFTERS 4

SAMANTHA LEAL

Fated Mate Daddy Bear

Copyright ©2019 by Samantha Leal

https://www.totallyromancebooks.com/samantha-leal

Join the Totally Romance Facebook Group!

CONTENTS

Chapter 1   1
Chapter 2   7
Chapter 3   16
Chapter 4   24
Chapter 5   34
Chapter 6   41
Chapter 7   49
Chapter 8   59
Chapter 9   66
Chapter 10   70
Chapter 11   80
Chapter 12   90
Chapter 13   99
Chapter 14   105
Chapter 15   114
Chapter 16   121

CHAPTER 1

The search party had been combing the mountainside since the early hours of the morning. They had witnessed the dawn fog rolling in, the chill in the air, and the sun finally rising in the distance. They had watched from their various vantage points, wondering if this would keep happening in their part of the world or they would soon be doomed to eternal darkness.

Anson raised his hands and hooked them behind his head as he looked out across the mountain at the magnificent scene ahead of him. He had spent his morning climbing with the rest of his pack, surveying the forests and woodlands, checking and prepping for the next wave of terror to head their way.

They all hoped it wouldn't happen, but these shifter boys knew their stuff. And they could all feel it.

With the cold air of October, Bridge Hollow was also gripped with another fresh set of threats. Somewhere, a storm was brewing for them, and they had to be ready. For what could easily pose as a sleepy mountain town to the outside world, they sure had a lot going on when it came to drama. They may have had a reputation for their strange phenomena, but the tourists came in droves to feel excitement, not necessarily to find something paranormal. Since the beginning of the year, however, Bridge Hollow had been coming up trumps in that department.

The whole town was morphing before the resident's very eyes.

Each day brought uncertainty and more fear. And now, it was up to the shifter packs of the town to make sure everyone stayed safe.

* * *

His fellow pack members were a few hundred meters away sniffing the air, and Anson watched them. Even in their human form the way they picked up scents was heightened, and they had used it to their advantage since they had begun their search.

"What do you think?" Ryder asked him as they looked out at the snow-capped mountain. "Are we going up, or back down?"

Anson looked over his shoulder to the rest of the pack. If he was honest, he didn't think there was any need to go higher.

"The dragons would have found it by now," he said as he looked to the clouds and the top of the mountain range. "They spend the majority of their time hidden away up there... Surely, they would have noticed something."

Ryder nodded.

The two men turned and began to walk quickly down the slope toward the rest of the pack and then on to town. After all their searching and switching shifts with the wolves, still no one had found what they were looking for. And now, they were all beginning to get weary. For weeks, they had been searching for answers, for a place they were yet to understand but knew they had to find.

And it had eluded them every time.

Bridge Hollow had turned on all of them. There was danger waiting in the wings, ready to seize them. But the bears and wolves were prepared. They had to be. If they didn't stay two steps ahead, then they were all doomed.

The pack delved into the thick woodland as they made their way down to town, and they all stopped and pricked their ears as they came to the site of where the last tragedy had happened. Anson felt the chill roll through him, right down to the very center of his bones. It still felt like only a moment had passed since the vampire had waited for them. He had been a threat so wild and frightening, none of them had seen him coming. True evil had found its way to them, and even though they had defeated it this time, they knew more was to come.

"Come on," Anson said as he looked away from the clearing in the trees where the showdown had taken place. Even though it had been weeks before, he could still see the charred scar on the ground where they had killed the vampire. And he didn't want to remember it all over again.

He carried on walking with his shoulders held back and his head high. He was a strong bear, a protector of this town, and now that he had a taste of what was to come, he was certain he wasn't going to let his life be shattered.

He had too much to lose.

As they reached the beginnings of the log cabins and the last mountain roads that gave way to the more major route into town, Anson felt a rush of warmth and relief.

This was home.

It always would be.

He smiled as he ran a big, rough hand through his shaggy, brown hair and he thought of all he had to love here. His wonderful little world at home that he would die for.

He turned back and raised his hand to wave at Ryder and the other bears and then sloped off down his street to his cabin.

It was time for him to call it a day, to leave his brotherhood behind, but return to his other family. The one that had his whole heart.

His boots scuffed the ground as he walked past his red truck, and he laughed at the crumpled pink bike with its training wheels that had been abandoned in a pile by the front door. Already from inside he could hear the laughing and girly voice of his daughter and it made his eyes water with happiness.

He reached for the handle and opened it, and as he stepped inside his home, he saw her turn and her eyes glint as she ran to him.

"Daddy!" she called as she scrambled down the hallway and jumped into his arms. He held her tight as she wrapped her arms around his neck and nuzzled her face in the stubbly beard on his chin.

"Hey, little darling," he said warmly as he looked into the kitchen to see his old aunt smiling back at him.

"I missed you," the little girl said as she hugged him tighter, and he held her there, never knowing relief like it. He was so glad to be back there with Heidi.

Every time he left the house to go on the hunt and search, he always feared he would never come home to her. And every time he did, he felt a new sense of gratitude.

He placed her down and they walked back to the kitchen, hand in hand. Heidi was excited to show him all the crafts she had made that day.

"And look at this!" she said with a beaming smile as she pulled out a paper plate with a face made of macaroni.

His old Aunt Nora laughed.

"The old ones are the best," Aunt Nora said with glistening eyes. "I remember making those with you when you were a boy."

Anson winked and laughed.

"You made one of these, Daddy?" Heidi asked with a grin.

"I sure did," he said as he knelt and took the plate from her.

It was funny how some traditions stayed the same. And he was so grateful to have his aunt by his side to help him on this crazy journey as a single father. She had always been there for him, but she was getting on in her years, and he could see the glint in her eyes was fading.

"Are you all right?" he asked her as he stood and rested his hand on his shoulder.

Aunt Nora smiled and nodded.

"I'm just tired," she said. "She takes it out of me."

Heidi was already jumping around in the living area and dancing along to a music video on TV. Anson knew the feeling. He had never known anyone to have as much energy as Heidi, and he could see how his aunt would be worn out after a few hours with her, never mind a full day.

"Put your feet up," he told her. "I'll sort us all out some food and you can spend the night. No need to be driving back when we have two spare rooms going to waste."

"Okay, son," she smiled. "I'll do that."

Even though she was his mother's older sister, she had always called him son, and Anson was just fine with that. When he had been growing up, it had always felt like he had two mothers anyway.

"But you could do with a woman around here to do the cooking, you know..." she winked and gave a little grin.

Anson rolled his eyes and laughed.

"I'm not getting into that again," he said. "You know I'm just fine on my own."

His aunt raised her hands in surrender and turned to look out the window, and Anson tried to push the thought out of his mind.

The thought of letting someone in after all he had been through just didn't seem possible. He had too much to focus on with Heidi, and he would never put her happiness at risk. No one would ever be good enough. He rolled out his shoulders and slapped his palms together.

"Right then," he said as he turned and opened the cupboards. "Let's get this show on the road."

He helped Heidi set the table, and then he heated soup on the stove and sliced some fresh, crusty bread. When they all sat to eat, he once again felt a rush of relief pass over him, and he was thankful for being safe with the people he loved.

He knew he had a dangerous time ahead. But he would do whatever it took to ensure his family was safe. He was a bear of Bridge Hollow, and he was more than ready for the challenge.

CHAPTER 2

*K*rystal turned the envelope over in her hands and bit her bottom lip with nervousness. Since the letter had arrived, she had known this moment was going to come, and yet, she still felt herself wracked with dread as she sat outside the border of town and thought twice about whether she should actually continue.

Bridge Hollow.

A world she had long tried to avoid but one that had come looking for her anyway. She let her eyes flit over the details on the welcome sign. At the bears and wolves, the crescent moon in the corner and the autumn leaves that had once been etched in orange but had long faded to a dull nothingness. She had always wondered if it would appear like in her vague childhood memories, and it seemed to be mostly the same so far, just a little washed out and jaded.

She sighed and looked back at the envelope. The engine was still running, and she knew she couldn't put entering town off much longer, but she had to take a moment to revisit why she had come here in the first place.

Her long, slender fingers flipped open the back of the

envelope and slowly slid out the piece of paper that had been tucked neatly inside. It was just one page, folded in half, and when she opened it and looked at the short but important message scrawled in the familiar handwriting, she couldn't help feeling a wave of warmth roll through her. But she didn't know if it was affection or fear.

I need you, Krystal. The store can't be left alone, and I must travel. I will explain when you arrive...
Aunt Beau x

It was short and sweet; to the naked eye, it would probably seem completely innocent, but Krystal knew different.

She had seen the news and read the online articles and theories that had been circulating. Bridge Hollow had a well-known past, a reputation for being mystical and magic, for paranormal phenomena that no one could explain. And recently, since the beginning of the year, things had been ramped to the max.

And now she had a letter from her aunt asking her to come to town and watch over her affairs while she *traveled*. This could only mean one thing... Beau was worried... and she was heading out of town to look for help.

Krystal scratched the back of her neck and let her eyes scan the sweeps and curves of Beau's ornate handwriting. It was unmistakably hers' she had known it before she had even opened the letter when it arrived two weeks before.

Now, Krystal had to have faith. She had packed her life in the city, and headed back to the place she had once called home. But that was a time long ago, back when she still had a mother and some kind of family-life. Now, she was out in the world alone with only her eccentric aunt who still worked in the town that had almost driven her mother mad.

Krystal threw the envelope on the passenger seat beside her and took a deep breath. She had spent so much of her life being afraid of this place. Her mother had warned her of the craziness that could happen in this part of the world. She knew about the shifter men, how they were to be avoided at all costs. Her mother had told her how brutish they could be, how they were all bad news. They were emotionally immature and physically frightening, and for that reason, Krystal had vowed never to go back to this place. She had said she didn't want to get drawn into a society that could damage or destroy her… and yet, here she was. About to drive straight back in, after twenty years, and confront everything she had always been warned against.

She hoped her mother would understand and that she wasn't turning in her grave.

She gripped the steering wheel and pressed her foot against the gas. As she eased off the bumpy roadside and returned to the smooth asphalt, she only had one thought running through her mind…

How was she going to feel when she finally saw this place all over again?

It had been such a long time; she had been just a child when she and her mother had left. And now, she was back… and she was about to see it as an adult for the first time.

She took a deep breath and kept moving forward.

She had come this far. There was no backing out now.

The shop door was bright purple, as was the awning covering the immediate stretch of pavement outside the store and providing shelter for the knickknacks and items for sale that were out there.

Krystal stopped the car and looked at it. A smile forced itself to her lips, and she found herself nodding and laughing. It was so typically her aunt. The paranormal store in the center of Bridge Hollow. She must make a fortune with the tourists, it looked like it had been freshly painted, and Krystal could see the place was well maintained and loved.

She turned off the engine and gathered her thoughts. When she was a child, she spent a lot of time there, but now, she realized she didn't much remember the store. She had vague memories of running around lots of dusty book-shelves, the hot and spicy scent of incense lingering in the air, the way there were wind chimes in each and every corner that sang with the whistle of the wind as it rolled through from the windows and front doorway. But the finer details, the way the place had looked and the layout, were completely lost on her. She didn't know what she was about to walk into, she just hoped it was somewhere that wouldn't make her miss her mother more than she could bear.

She stepped out of the car and locked it behind her. She gripped her purse strap firmly in her fist and then she stepped out on Main Street to cross to the other side. As she got closer to the doorway, her heart began to pick up pace, but then, she felt herself begin to relax. She could already smell incense, and little tufts of smoke were drifting out of mini cauldrons that had been placed on the tables outside.

"That smells like home," she said with a smile as she reached for the door handle.

She had barely grazed it with her fingertips when the door flew open and an elegant lady with silver hair came into view with her arms held open wide. She swept Krystal into them and pulled her close, and as they embraced, Krystal felt tears prick the corner of her eyes.

"Aunt Beau," she whispered as they held each other.

"Krystal," Beau beamed.

They hugged in the doorway for what felt like an eternity before both women laughed and separated. The two went into the store.

Krystal's eyes widened as she scanned the room and it all started to come flooding back to her. It was as if she had subconsciously yearned for this place and deliberately blocked out the magical wonder of it. She looked at the lofty ceilings and the beams that ran across with fairy lights entwined around them. There were shelves of books in rows on one side, but they seemed so much smaller than she had remembered them. She looked at the crystals on display and for sale, she looked at the tarot cards and the dedicated area at the back of the store where Beau must do her readings. It was all so familiar, and yet there was something not quite right. As she saw the details and the memories came back to her, she was sure the store she remembered had been bigger. It had been more of a library with a separate area at the front for selling occult items, but this place had less space for books.

"It seems so different," she said. "I don't remember it being like this... I feel like my mind is playing tricks on me."

Beau smiled, and Krystal couldn't help noticing how smooth and unlined her skin was. With her long silver hair, from the back she could have easily been mistaken for an old woman, but Beau couldn't have been any older than forty. She was her mother's younger sister and had always been the more eccentric of the two. She wore a deep purple shawl and her blue eyes seemed to glow against the paleness of her skin and hair.

"It is different," Beau said. "But I suppose it has been a long time since you and your mother left..."

"Twenty years," Krystal said. "I haven't been back since Mom wanted to move."

"Well, I know," she half laughed. "I've had to visit you every year since."

Krystal gave a mischievous smile.

"Mom didn't want me to come back," she said. "She hated it here."

"Your mother was stubborn," Beau said warmly. "And I have the feeling you've likely inherited a lot of that."

Krystal laughed.

"So," Beau said as she sat at the counter and stirred a cup of herbal tea. "Would you like a cup?"

There was a small iron teapot next to a small mug and Krystal shrugged and nodded. She watched as Beau poured it for her and passed it her way. The scent of cinnamon and clove seemed to explode from the steam, and it made her long for candles and a roaring fire. She loved this time of year and coming back to Bridge Hollow was certainly expanding her love for Autumn and all that came with it.

"This is a completely different building," Beau said suddenly. "The store your mother and I opened when we were younger was on the other side of town."

Krystal felt her eyes widen with shock; that had been something she hadn't been expecting to hear.

"Wow," she said. "Really? How come?"

Beau shrugged her shoulders, and as Krystal let herself acclimatize to the place, she realized there were still boxes stacked in corners and toward the back of the room that hadn't been unpacked.

"You've moved in recently?" she asked.

Beau nodded.

"Only last week." She took a sip of her tea. "And I know the place is probably looking like a shabby mess, but what can you do."

"No," Krystal shook her head and looked back around the

place, "I can't believe you only moved in last week, it looks incredible."

"It still needs a lot of work," Beau admitted. "And I suppose I could be done in the next couple of weeks or so, if I didn't have to leave."

Finally, she made it to the subject Krystal had been eager to hear more about. It must have been ten months since she had last seen her aunt. Even though Krystal hadn't been back to Bridge Hollow, she had regularly met with her aunt halfway between there and the city, or Beau had come to stay with her. With her mother gone, the two had remained close, and Krystal would do anything for her, and vice versa. But Beau hadn't wanted to tell Krystal what was going on in a letter, and now that she had arrived in town, she couldn't wait to hear the truth.

"What's going on?" Krystal asked as she sipped her tea. "You've got me here, but you're going to have to fill me in…"

Beau nodded and sighed.

"I don't even know where to begin," she said. "I suppose I could start with the fact that this place isn't everything your mother always led you to believe."

"Oh, great," Krystal laughed. "Do continue…"

Beau laughed too and she reached out and squeezed Krystal's hand. It felt good for them to be there together, and she realized how at ease she was there. She had spent so long trying to forget and ignore this place. Until she had received the letter, she had barely even considered what it would be like to come back and really throw herself into Bridge Hollow life.

"Have you seen the news?" Beau asked. "The theories online?"

"I've seen some," she said with a shrug. "Strange weather, missing people… that's the official story on the news, anyway… Online, though…"

"Yes," Beau said with a raised brow. "Online, it's a different story."

"It's been kept relatively quiet?" Krystal asked as she stirred her cup and listened to the ting of the spoon on the side.

"For good reason," Beau said. "No one really understands what is going on."

"And where are you going?" Krystal didn't like skirting around subjects. She had to be tough with losing her mom at such a young age, and now that she was confident in her own skin, she wasn't about to let her aunt be vague with her when she had dropped her whole life to help her.

"I need to find some help," she said. "I need to travel to Europe."

"What's in Europe?"

"An old friend."

A chill rolled up Krystal's spine.

"He's an expert in this sort of thing," Beau said. "But for now, I just need you to look after the store, keep us ticking over, enjoy yourself here, and get to know your heritage."

She looked at Krystal hopefully, but she didn't know if she was convinced.

"Are you sure that's the only reason?"

Beau threw her head back and laughed.

"Isn't that one big enough?" she asked with wide eyes. "I need to find an expert who might be able to help us out here. The government supposedly has sent people along in the past who have looked into climate change, the mineral levels in the soil and some of the strange happenings, but so far, no one has been of any use."

"And why does it fall on you to go?" Krystal asked.

"Because I'm the one with the connections," she said with a roll of her eyes. "It's nothing to worry about, dear," she laughed. "I'll be home in a few weeks."

Krystal shrugged again and sighed. She had known when she had trekked out of the city and came across to the mountains that she would be walking into riddles, but at least her aunt was being as upfront as she could.

"Okay," she smiled. "No problem."

"I don't trust anyone else," Beau said. "You're my family… you understand why I have to ask?"

"Of course, I do," Krystal said as she wrapped her arms around her aunt. "And you know I would never let you down."

"Thank you," Beau said as she gave her an extra squeeze of affection. "Now, let's get your things upstairs and unpacked, and I can cook us something to eat."

"You live here?" Krystal asked with a raised brow as her eyes traveled to the ceiling.

"Perks of the job," Beau shrugged. "Get the shop space and the three floors above. It's a big building. Wait 'til you see it!"

She gripped Krystal's hand and dashed to the front of the store to close down for the day. Krystal watched as she extinguished candles and incense, and then she helped to bring in some of the tables and for sale items from the sidewalk. When Beau turned the sign on the door to CLOSED, and they locked the door for the day, it was as if she had actually done a full day's work herself. Krystal was suddenly exhausted from the drive and all the information she had to process.

"Come on then," her aunt said with a grin. "Time to show you your new home for the next few weeks."

What Krystal had yet to tell her was now that she was back, she had no intention of leaving. She just hoped Bridge Hollow was going to welcome her home with open arms.

CHAPTER 3

Anson watched from the window of his truck as Heidi ran up the steps to school with her friends and was welcomed at the door by their teacher. He smiled and waved as she turned back to wave at him, and he felt good in the knowledge that she was safe and occupied for another day.

He had been up all night working and his head was pounding, but he knew he couldn't just abandon the rest of his life and responsibilities because there was shifter business to attend to. They may have been his brotherhood, but he had a livelihood to run too. He had properties to oversee, building projects to help map out, and a town to keep on its feet with the festival that was getting closer and closer by the second. When it reached this time of year in town, it was always a reminder that the annual festival was well on its way. When October had passed and November came rolling in, it was only a matter of days before the tourists began to descend, and that was if they hadn't already come by Halloween.

The bell for class rang out and once he saw the doors

were closed and locked, and Heidi was most certainly safely inside, he finally edged the truck away from the sidewalk and drove toward the center of town.

He crept along the traffic of Main Street with his window still down and took in the sights and sounds of his home. This was one of his favorite times of the day, and he could already smell the fresh bread and cakes being cooked in the bakery, the coffee and hot chocolate being served up in the cafes and coffee houses, and he could also smell Beau's incense drifting out from the paranormal store in the middle of town. He had to smile. If there was one thing he could count on when it came to this place, it was that the locals loved it as much as he did, and for that reason, he was happy to give them decent rates when it came to their leases on commercial property.

He pulled the truck to a halt when he found a spare place to park, and paid the meter before he headed to his buildings. For years, Anson and his family had owned a vast majority of the commercial space along Main Street. He was from one of the original shifter bear families that had settled in Bridge Hollow, and they had built and acquired much of the land around the area. Now, Anson had the responsibility of helping the locals run their businesses. He promised to keep rates low so they could continue to thrive, and when Beau, the lady who ran the paranormal store, had come to him asking for help when her last landlord had hiked the rent, he had been more than happy to oblige. Even throwing in a place to live with it and letting her have the entire four floors of the building.

He would be lying if he said he didn't want to help her more than others around town. He knew that if there was anyone who could help him and his brotherhood when it came to the strange happenings of Bridge Hollow, then it would be Beau. She had been in town for as long as he could remember, and he had seen how the tourists flocked to her for mystical palm readings and to hear their fortunes. She seemed to have her finger on the pulse of the town, and it was clear she had the respect of many of the shifters in the area, some of them even traveling to her to hear their fates.

It had been bad luck and a clear sign to all of them when even she hadn't seen the evil that had come to the town all those weeks before, and even she was stumped as to what was causing these strange phenomena.

He stopped when he reached the store and ran a hand through his hair. It was another beautiful day, and he had a lot on his plate, but while it was such a stunning morning, he was determined to let himself enjoy it and move at a slower pace than normal. He owed it to himself to at least try not to drive himself mad by working too hard.

He opened the door and a bell chimed above his head. The now smoky darkness of the store came into view, and he was still surprised at how different it was to what it had been like before. When he had first leased it to Beau the space had been a completely blank canvas. The walls had been white, the floor light wood, and the beams above them were dark and bold in contrast to the rest of the clinical nature of the white room. Now, the beams were glistening with fairy lights, tapestries hung on the walls and half of them had been painted bright colors. Lush, fur rugs were spread out across the floors and the whole room popped with colors and glistening crystals and orbs. Candles were lit and incense swirled in the air, wind chimes tinged and low music was playing. It was like stepping into an Aladdin's cave, and it completely brought back to him how much he loved going into the old paranormal store when he was a kid, when Beau and her sister had run it across the other side of town.

"Beau?" he called as he closed the front door behind him, and the bell chimed again.

The store seemed completely empty, but he stepped further inside and began to look at some of the spines of the books that were lined along the shelves, tightly packed like sardines.

THE PSYCHIC WORLD... TAROT FOR BEGINNERS... WITCHCRAFT AND MAGICAL HISTORY OF NORTHERN AMERICA... CRYSTAL HEALING... DIVINATION...

The titles were all so enchanting and made him stop and take notice, and he was just about to reach up and pull the history book from the shelf when he heard the slam of a door somewhere out the back and the hurried rush of footsteps. He dropped his hand and was about to shout hello to Beau when a voice he didn't recognize came first.

"Good morning!" A bright, cheerful girl's voice rang out from the back of the store. "Can I help you?"

He spun around on the spot and his eyes found her. She was close to the back of the room, a cardboard box hitched up under her arm and resting on her hip. She smiled at him, and her long black hair was right down the length of her waist, curled and thick. Her eyes were blue, and they shone out at him, and he noticed the curve of silver gripped tightly to one of her nostrils.

A piercing... Spunky... he thought.

He smiled and crossed his big, muscular arms over his chest and then took a step toward her.

"New girl?" he asked.

She narrowed her eyes and stepped in closer, the smile still playing on her lips, but her guard most definitely up.

"Maybe," she said as she set the box down on the countertop next to the cash register. "And who are you? You certainly don't look like the kind of clientele we usually get in here?"

He cocked his head to the side with confusion. Who the

hell was this girl, and what the fuck did she know about him and the kind of people who came into this store? He had never seen her before in his entire life and she was busting his balls in the building he *owned*…

She was in for a whole world of trouble.

He grinned and laughed.

"I'm here to see Beau," he said finally, deciding to soften up. He didn't want to get this girl fired on what could easily be her first day. "I'm the landlord…"

Her face fell a little and then she shook her head and laughed.

"Sorry," she said as she took a step forward and held out her hand. "I'm Krystal, Beau's niece."

As she stepped toward him, a surge of energy hit him, and he found himself locked in on her eyes. The blue was so deep and intense, he almost gasped. His heart was raging in his chest and a tingle rolled up his spine. It all happened so fast to him, but it was almost as if it were playing out in slow motion. As Krystal stepped toward him and he caught her scent, he felt himself open up, a place inside him came alive and the animal inside him was beginning to stir.

He instinctively took a step back and felt his jaw sag open.

What was happening to him?

A tremble rolled through him, but the feeling was divine. It was something he could easily become addicted to. It was warm and electrifying but there was also something very calming within it too.

Surely, this couldn't be happening…

He had heard others in his pack, and many elders talk about the day they found their fated mate. The one true other half of their soul and the person they were supposed to spend the rest of their life with. But Anson had gone through his days pushing it well out of his mind… But this feeling… it was just like they had all described.

He cleared his throat and took a step back. His mind a muddle of bewilderment.

When the world went back to moving at a regular pace, he registered the look of confusion on her face and she slowly dropped her hand, aware that he wasn't going to shake it.

She looked wounded and bruised, and he went to speak, but didn't have a clue what to say.

"Okay…" she half whispered.

"I'm Anson," he said to break the silence. "I'm just here for the rent."

And now he was coming across like a total dick. But he couldn't understand what was happening to him. He had never felt anything like that before, as if his whole body had suddenly gone into overdrive. He felt his senses heighten and his heart was still raging, his skin tingled, and his cock pulsed with desire, he had to look away from her and he had to get out of there fast.

She was looking at him as if he were insane, either that or she was incredibly offended.

"I don't know anything about any rent," she said sternly as she crossed her arms over her chest.

Her eyes were searching him as if she were trying to figure him out, and a flicker of realization seemed to flash across her face before she stepped backward, turned to face the other way and walked to the back of the room and behind the counter so she could be as far away from him as possible.

"Well, it's due every month on this date," he said. "Where's Beau?"

The girl looked momentarily worried, but then she sighed and reached for her cell phone.

"She's gone away for a few weeks," she said finally as she seemed to be hurriedly typing a text. "She flew out of here and I guess in all the rush she forgot to mention that. I'm sure it'll be sorted though, so just give me a couple of days to figure it out."

She was now refusing to look him in the eye, and he took a step back, feeling the hostility toward him. Not that it was her fault, he was the one being a total jerk.

What the fuck is happening? He thought as he reached the door and went for the handle.

"I'll call back then," he said as he cleared his throat. "No rush... I mean... Just speak to her."

"Sure," Krystal said as she watched him leave with a scowl across her face.

He lunged through the door and let it slam behind him, the bell and the wind chimes all going crazy as he went and he strode off down the street as fast as he could, not looking back. When he was a safe distance away and his heart had returned to normal, he looked at his hands and it were as if he should be able to see the blood thumping through his veins. There was nothing to see, just his regular palms, but his whole inside was on fire. His body was reacting to something, and it was both exhilarating and frightening.

He ran a hand through his hair and took a deep breath as he leaned back against a building down an alleyway just off Main Street. He had lived his whole life never experiencing anything like this, but it was hard to ignore. The girl, Krystal, with her piercing blue eyes, long black hair and sexy nose ring... She had done more than caught his eye when he had walked into the store just now.

Her scent had enchanted him.

"Fuck," he whispered as he closed his eyes. "No... No... No..."

His Aunt Nora's words echoed in his mind and he shook

his head and refused to acknowledge them. Today was just another day, and he certainly wasn't going to let himself be tempted by the new girl in town which just so happened to be one of the psychic's nieces.

He was mad a himself for not having more self-control.

He didn't want a woman in his life. He already had enough on his plate looking after Aunt Nora and Heidi. He had a brotherhood and a serious business, and the town was in the grips of a sinister turmoil they didn't yet know the full implications of.

He waited until he had calmed and then shook his head again, moving out of the alley and back on Main Street. He wasn't going to let that strange feeling throw him off course today, he had too much to do.

Sexy shop girl or no sexy shop girl. He was pushing her out of his mind and getting back to work.

CHAPTER 4

Krystal sat at the register cradling her cup of takeout coffee and her slice of carrot cake. The scowl was still fixed firmly on her face, and no amount of caffeine and sugar was going to clear it any time soon.

Anson.

He had seriously pissed her off, but he had also piqued her interest because she had marked his card a few moments after he walked in.

Anson was a shifter.

He had acted such a tough guy and he had been so rude, and it hadn't taken Krystal long to figure out why. He was an immature animal, one with no emotional maturity, and one that only focused on one thing… mating and acting like a total savage.

She shuddered.

He hadn't been quite what she had been expecting when she had come back to town and had made peace with the fact that she was going to be around shifter men. She had thought she would have known instinctively the second he had walked in the door, but it had taken her a good few moments, and she wasn't sure if he hadn't acted so bizarrely if she would have seen it at all.

He had looked like a man. A huge, hulking beast of a man with muscles to die for, sure, but a man… not an animal. He had deep brown eyes, shaggy hair and a gorgeous beard that made her bones ache, but he hadn't been as repulsive has she had thought they might be. Everything she had ever heard about shifter men had been negative. Her mother had known them well when she had lived in Bridge Hollow, and she had always told her how dangerous they were and that they were totally bad news.

Well, he was rude, that was one thing that was certain.

He had no manners, he looked like a hulking mountain man, and he had run out without even saying bye.

And Krystal had been in a bad mood ever since.

She stabbed at her piece of cake with the plastic fork the coffee house had given her, and she tasted one more tiny bit before she pushed it away and sighed.

She had been in town for a week now minding the store, and that had been the first time she had come in contact with, what she was pretty sure was, a shifter. In fact, it was the first time she had spoken with anyone except the patrons of the store and the people who worked in the coffee house. She had wandered around town without being noticed and she put it down to the fact she must just blend in as a tourist. Not many of the locals had been into the store, most of the time, for this week at least, it had been tourists looking for some kind of magical souvenir to take home, and with Beau being away, no bookings had been taken for tarot readings or other forms of divination.

She sipped her coffee and realized that her mind kept drifting back to Anson, even though she was trying her hardest not to think about him. He had been such a big presence when he had come to the store, she had almost felt him before she had heard or seen him, and it was as if she just knew someone had come in. She had been out back in the store room and hadn't heard the bell ting, or anyone call to her, but she had felt the energy of someone else in the same space as her, and it had made her dash to the front of the shop. She had almost been afraid they were be being robbed, as if her intuition was kicking in. But when she saw him browsing the mystical book section, she could see that he was a customer and not a thief.

Not even a customer, she corrected herself with a cringe. *The owner of the building.*

She tapped her phone to make the screen come alive and there was still no reply from her aunt. As soon as he had appeared and asked for money, she had texted Beau to ask her if she had left an envelope anywhere, or if there was a bank account she could access to transfer it across to him. Her aunt had been pretty good at keeping her updated on her travels, and she had arrived in Germany the day after she had left Bridge Hollow after only having to take two flights.

When Beau had left, she had briefed her on the person she was looking for. He was an expert in parapsychology and the spirit world, and Beau was beginning to become convinced that the happenings of Bridge Hollow could be connected to an accident that had happened there almost a hundred years ago and it was the spirits of the people who had died that were coming back and trying to punish the town for forgetting them.

Krystal didn't know what to think, but she could see the determination and urgency in Beau's eyes, and she had wanted to find her friend in Europe to see if he had any theories of his own. It was typical for her that this man was eccentric and had shunned modern technology, choosing to live out his days in practical isolation in the middle of a forest.

And now Krystal was back in Bridge Hollow after twenty years, leaving when she had only been seven years old, and she had just had her first encounter with a shifter.

"I wonder what kind," she found herself saying with a little smile before she shook her head and made the thoughts go away.

She sipped the rest of her coffee and got to her feet, she had plenty she could be doing around the store before closing time, and the afternoon was passing by quickly. She looked over her shoulder at the selection of boxes that were still left to be unpacked and she decided she would make the executive decision to start decorating the place a little more. If she did a good job, she hoped her aunt may keep her on once she had returned.

As it hit 6pm, Krystal hadn't even realized it had gotten so late. No one had come into the store for hours, and when she looked outside, she realized the sun was low in the sky and dusk was rolling in. She shivered and rubbed her arms to warm herself up, and then she made her way to the front of the store and began to collect the items outside on the sidewalk, the chairs and tables, sandwich board with the store logo, and the little items she had put out for sale.

She thought she could feel a pair of eyes on her, and when she looked up, she noticed a big truck was parked on the opposite side of the street, and a couple of men were standing and talking by the side of it. She intuitively knew it was him from the size of him. Even though he wasn't underneath the streetlight and it was dark over there, she could tell it was Anson.

She had managed to block him out of her mind for the rest of the afternoon, keeping herself so busy by unpacking boxes and getting sorted, but it was as if someone wasn't going to let her forget him that easily.

He was chatting to his friend and they both looked like they were from a different world. They were both so big and muscular, they were incredible to look at and it made her swallow nervously.

These men were seriously fucking sexy.

She hadn't bargained for that when she had returned to her hometown.

They must do all kinds of bad things for her mom to warn her off them so vehemently when she had been alive.

He turned and his eyes caught hers instantly, as if he could feel her standing there watching him. A smile quickly flickered across his lips and she found herself smiling, too, but then it was as if they both realized at the same time that they shouldn't be acknowledging each other, and Krystal quickly forced her smile to drop, quickly followed by his, before she turned and continued carrying everything back inside the store.

She could feel his eyes on her, but luckily she had managed to get everything inside, and without letting herself look at him again, she flipped the sign to CLOSED, locked the door and turned off the main light at the front of the shop before she scuttled to the back.

When she opened the storeroom door and went inside her heart was pounding and breath came quickly. Her palms were slick with sweat and she had tingling skin.

"Jeez," she breathed as she fanned her face. Her nipples were hard and her pussy ached. "What the fuck was that...?"

She waited for a moment until she felt like she could breathe normally again, and then she rolled out her shoulders and slipped back out of the storeroom and locked it behind her. She flicked off the rest of the lights in the store and went out the back hallway toward the staircase that led to the split-level apartment above.

She was already in love with the apartment, and she had really felt at home since she had arrived. Her aunt hadn't truly been living there, but she had clearly known she was going to need the space for someone, and so she had taken Anson up on his offer for the extra floors. They had been empty anyway, and Krystal had already decided that when she told her aunt she was going to be staying in Bridge Hollow, she would offer to pay the landlord extra for the space.

She loved slipping the key into the door and stepping inside. There was something so light and airy about the place, and she felt instantly safe as if it had been made just for her. The building was old, and the ceilings were high in every room, but this apartment had been refurbed so that the floor above was showing in the main living area with a mezzanine level balconied and looking out above her. She liked it up there the best, she had set it up as her main living space and it felt like she was in a secret treehouse when she was in there. She had a comfy couch, beanbags on the floor, and all the books she had managed to fit in her cases when she had driven into town.

She still didn't know what her aunt was going to make of her wanting to stay full-time in Bridge Hollow. But over the past few years, Krystal had really felt the distance between them. After she lost her mom when she was eighteen, she had tried her absolute best to make it in the world without any family close by. But over time, it had started to take its toll and she had begun to feel incredibly lonely. She saw people going off to their parents' homes on the weekend for Sunday lunches and to spend time at lake houses, and Krystal had been sitting alone in a studio apartment in a bustling city that had made her feel isolated.

She had been scared stiff about returning to Bridge Hollow, but she couldn't say it hadn't already been on her mind before she had received Beau's letter. It had been something she had been toying with for at least two years. Every time she and Beau met for a weekend away, or Beau came to her for Christmas or other holidays, she almost asked her every time, but had always lost her nerve at the last minute. It was almost as if she was waiting for a sign and for the right time.

When the letter had come, asking her to go back, she knew there was no denying it any longer. She had been scared to make the decision, and it had been tough saying goodbye to her friends, but they were all settling down and getting married, and she had been seeing less and less of them over the months. She had hated her job and been looking for a fresh start, and she had never connecting with any of the men she had dated in the city. They had all been too pretentious and stuck up, and she always felt a draw back to her old hometown. She just needed the validation to be able to make the move, so she didn't feel so bad on her wonderful mother. For Beau to ask her to come back though, that was what she had needed. She may not have told her yet, but while she had been gone, Krystal had been moving things bit by bit up from the trunk in her car and into the apartment, hoping she would be able to soon call it her permanent home.

She finally felt as if she belonged to something, and she certainly had yearned for this place, even if her memories from her childhood were scattered and weak. She had settled in fast, and she was loving her cozy nights in the apartment, she loved working in the store, and once she felt a bit more confident around town, she knew was going to love going out and hitting up the bars and nightspots and making some real friends too. She didn't realize how much she had hated the city until she had found herself here, and she just hoped her mom wouldn't be disappointed with her for wanting to come back.

She smiled and reached for the silver locket at her neck which contained a small picture of her mother. She always had it close to her heart, and she had tried her best to stay away, but now she was back, she knew it meant she was finally moving on and becoming willing to take charge of her own life. And for the first time in a long, long time, she was feeling happy and content just in her own skin.

Her cell phone beeped and she picked it up and looked down at the screen. She had a new message from Beau, and she opened it and began to read…

B: Sorry, darling! Yes, of course, I totally forgot to tell you, the cash for Anson is in the safe in the basement. I'll call you tomorrow with the details to get into it, I don't want to send them over these airwaves, you never know who's jotting things down. I'm leaving for the forest tomorrow and I have good faith that my old friend is still in his cabin living in perfect and tranquil simplicity.

Going to bed now, it's very late here. I love you. Aunt B x

Krystal smiled and laughed. Her Aunt Beau was so funny at times. She was eccentric and loud, jolly and elegant, if she could grow up to be exactly like her, then she would be happy. Her and her mother had been similar, but Beau had definitely got the crazy gene while her mother had been more pragmatic.

She set the phone down and stretched before she wandered up the stairs, across the mezzanine level, and into one of the rooms that led off it and into her bedroom.

She still hadn't unpacked many of her things in there for

fear she would be told no by her aunt or by Anson, but she knew her aunt wouldn't want her to leave Bridge Hollow now she was home, it was more just the logistics of where she would live. If there weren't enough hours for her in the store, then she would have to look for something else, and she didn't know how Anson would feel about the apartment being sublet, even if it did mean there would be a trusted person on the premises at night.

She flopped down on her bed and lay looking at the ceiling. She really had felt strange since she had met him. His name and his eyes and the way he had glared at her had been piercing through her mind every five seconds. She felt excitement when she remembered him, when the vision of him crossed her mind, she felt every part of herself tingle with anticipation. She had never felt anything like it, as if she were both nervous of him, but also drawn to him and unable to shake him away.

She rolled to her side, gripped her pillow, and pulled it to her. She had come back to this town with a hope of starting her life again in a new place, even if it was one she had lived in before. She had hoped to find a job she was passionate about, and she had hoped to find some closure on her own demons, ones that had been unfortunately passed down to her by the incredible woman who had raised her. But now she was here, she was feeling things she hadn't expected.

She hadn't thought once about the social side. And she certainly hadn't considered the fact she may meet a shifter and be instantly attracted to him the way she had been to Anson.

"Attracted to him…?" she said the words out loud as the thought formed in her mind. "Holy hell… Am I?"

She squeezed her pillow tight and screamed into it, trying not to laugh. She felt excitement, she felt deliriously happy… but she also felt unbelievably conflicted.

Anson was nothing but trouble… it was clear for her to see. She had spent her whole life being warned off men like him and promising herself she would never find herself in this position. And yet here she was… and she knew she was screwed.

hen she woke in the morning, Krystal jumped out of bed feeling fresh as a daisy. She quickly showered and got dressed in a long black dress with ankle boots, fluffed up her hair into bouncing curls as she dried it and slicked on some dark lipstick. She laughed at herself in the mirror, realizing she had made herself look pretty gothic.

"Must be the season," she smiled as she spritzed on some perfume and then made her way down to the floor below to the kitchen where she made herself a big, steaming cup of coffee.

Her commute to work took her exactly half a minute from when she locked the door to the apartment. It was certainly a vast improvement on life in the city, she regularly had to be up well before 7am to shower and spend hours picking out a boring office outfit to make sure she looked as conservative as possible. She had always got the subway, it had been hot and stinky, too many people packed in together in dry, old air. If they broke down, it was a terrible way to start the day, and on the way home when she was dog tired and just wanting some peace and quiet, there was nothing worse than having to cram into another train and be hurtled across the underground. But here in Bridge Hollow, she jumped out of bed feeling fantastic at 8am, she took her time getting ready, dressed however the hell she wanted and even left in her nose ring, she skipped out the door at 9:15am and was still down and in the store within less than a minute and had time to set the ambience before she opened the door at 9:30. She was absolutely loving it, and she certainly hoped she would be able to continue living such a charmed life once her aunt returned.

She opened the store doors after the fairy lights and candles had been lit, she had set up the incense and was already dusting down the displays and unpacking the morning mail. She was aware that there was a new delivery arriving at around 10am, and she still had to set up the tables and chairs out the front along with the little cauldrons and other mystical wares for people to browse and hopefully be lured in by. She had never been so happy to come to work before, and she already felt like she was a part of the shop so much she was even tempted to offer to work for free if it meant she could keep hanging out there when Beau returned from her travels.

She sat down behind the counter and began to flick through a new magazine that had arrived, it was from a wholesaler in China who had started to make mass produced magical items. She crunched up her nose and shook her head. They all looked cute enough, but she was sure her aunt wouldn't want anything like that. A lot of the things she sold in her store were homemade by people close by or from small online boutiques. She also scoured vintage fairs, second hand shops and yard sales to find things that were completely unique and had a magic all their own.

She had just about finished her coffee when the store

telephone began to trill, and she picked up the receiver and held it to her ear.

"Morning Krystal!" Aunt Beau sang out before she had even had a chance to say hello.

"Hey!" Krystal said with delight. "How are you? It's good to hear your voice!"

"All is well," Beau said. Her voice still sounded so clear even though she was so far away, Krystal still found that completely mind-blowing. "I was just calling with the instructions for the safe," she said.

"Ahh, yes, so I can pay the *lovely Anson…*" Krystal tried to scowl but found herself smirking.

"Indeed," Beau's voice sounded rapt with delight and Krystal could sense she was smiling, even from all that way away.

"I was kidding," Krystal said. "He was rude."

"Who? Anson?" Her aunt sounded surprised. "Never!"

"Seriously," she said as she balanced the receiver between her shoulder and ear. "He came in and made me feel two inches high."

Her aunt laughed a little and then cleared her throat.

"He's a good man," she said seriously. "A very good man."

"Could have fooled me," Krystal said, but she was aware that even she was still smiling.

"Well, maybe he'll be in a better mood once you've paid him," Beau said, and Krystal could hear the teasing tone in her voice. "After all, we are a day late, and I don't like to leave a good landlord waiting."

"So… tell me," she said. "How do I get in this safe?"

"The keys to the basement are in the safety deposit box in the bottom drawer of the desk you're sitting at."

Krystal looked at the row of drawers underneath the countertop.

"Okay, I see it," she said.

"Go down into the basement and the safe is along the far wall, I haven't chance to sort out down there. In fact, I only ditched what I needed to and locked it, so it may be in a bit of a mess."

"That's okay, I'll see what I can move around."

"The code to the safe is 7676, nice and easy. There's an envelope in there and it'll say Anson on the front."

"Okay, thanks Aunt Beau," Krystal smiled as she reached down and slid open the bottom drawer. She saw the safety deposit box looking back up at her and she wrapped her free hand around it and pulled it up and on the top of the desk.

"No problem," his number is in top drawer too, I have a contact book in there."

"Sure," Krystal said as she quickly reached for the top drawer and opened it wide, she pushed papers around until she saw the little black book and her heart skipped a little beat.

"If you need anything else, just send me a message or call," Beau said. "I miss you darling! And thank you so much again for helping me out."

"I'm really enjoying it, no need to thank me," Krystal smiled. "I hope your travels are going well."

"I'll update you as soon as I can, but all good so far," Beau said. "I should say goodbye for now darling... but please don't be too hard on Anson... he's one of the good ones."

Krystal rolled her eyes but found herself agreeing.

If her mother and her aunt could only have agreed about that fact, then maybe Krystal never would have had to leave Bridge Hollow in the first place and live all those miserable lonely years in the city.

"Okay," she said. "Bye Aunt Beau."

"Goodbye darling," after Beau spoke the line clicked and then went dead.

Krystal smiled as she placed the receiver back down in

the cradle and flicked through the pages of the contact book. She didn't have to look far, Anson's number was right where she expected it, on the first page underneath the A's. She entered it into her cell phone contacts and then pushed the book back into the drawer before she opened the safety deposit box and pulled out the set of old long keys for the basement. They looked ancient, like something out of a horror movie, and she furrowed her brow and looked toward the door in the back.

"God knows what is down here," she said to herself ominously as she rose to her feet. "But I guess I better go and find out."

When the door to the basement creaked open, she instantly felt a rush of cold air at her ankles, which rose quickly up her legs to her knees and seemed to grip her heart.

She breathed out and was sure she could see the fog of breath in front of her, as if the temperature was below zero, but it was too dark to truly tell. She shivered on the spot and looked back behind her before she reached around in the darkness to find a light switch.

The rest of the building had been so warm and welcoming that this place seemed to be so far removed from it, as if she were stepping into another dimension. Krystal stepped to the top step and finally found the cord for the light, when she pulled it and the little bulb came zipping to life in front of her, she grimaced at the length of stairs ahead.

"Oh no," she said. "Talk about creepy."

The stairs were old and made of stone, thick and cracked and seemed to disappear down into the depths of the earth. It was clearly a massive basement, and she shuddered as she took the steps one at a time, trying not to grip to the rotting banister rail too tightly for fear of it crumbling in her hands.

When she reached the bottom, more darkness spread out in front of her and the light from the top of the stairs barely reached a meter in front of her. She let her hands trail around the wall, hoping to find another switch of some sort, but she had to keep moving further into the darkness and just hoped she would find a cord soon enough.

"Should have brought a flashlight," she said to herself, almost annoyed that she had been so stupid.

When she finally found another cord, she pulled it and the basement illuminated with a sizzle of the old bulb in the center of the room. She took a step back and gasped as she saw it, it was quite possibly the biggest basement she had ever seen and the cold down there was amplified by the stone floors and walls. It could have been used as a pantry, it was so dark and cold, and she rubbed her arms repeatedly to warm herself up.

She spotted the safe straight away among the boxes that had clearly been put there by her aunt, and she made her way to it and knelt in front of it. She entered the code and the door began to open and she was glad there wasn't a whole lot inside that she would have to sort through as the envelope for Anson was right there plain as day to see.

She gripped it in her cold fingers and then she locked the safe back and made her way to the stairs. She pulled the cord and the lights went out and then she ran up the stairs without looking back. All she could think about were all those scenes in scary movies where there is something lurking behind the victim in the darkness of the shadows, and she dived back out of the door and slammed it behind her before she turned the key in the lock.

"Fucking creepy," she gasped to herself as she pulled out the key and slipped it into her back pocket.

She looked at the envelope and then to the shop and then at the phone on the counter. She could put off calling him for the rest of the day, but it would be worse if he came looking for it. She had to do right by her aunt and give him a call and let him know the rent money was waiting.

She sat down and picked up her cell phone, and then she scrolled through her contacts to the newly entered number for Anson. With her heart pounding in her chest and her mouth going dry with nerves, she pressed dial.

CHAPTER 6

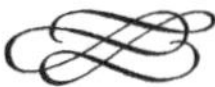

His morning had been as lovely as ever when he spent it with Heidi. She had gone off to school looking picture perfect, her pigtails swishing on either side of her head from Aunt Nora's wonderful hairdressing skills.

It was one of the things he had never been able to do. Pigtails were just so damned hard. Every time he tried, he seemed to get the hair caught up all wrong in the ties and it usually ended with Heidi sobbing that she wished she had a mommy around.

These were the moments that killed him inside. He could never tell Heidi her mother had abandoned them. That she had up and left when Heidi had only been a few months old. Some people liked to convince him she must not have been in her right mind, but he knew the truth. He had always known the truth about her. She was a selfish woman who didn't want to give up the party. He had done all he could to make their world a happy one, despite not being fully happy himself, but she just hadn't wanted him… and she certainly hadn't wanted Heidi. She had lived her life as normal while she had been pregnant, hanging around the bars of town every night, and even down at the dive bars on the highway. She was always drunk, she lied, and she cheated. When she had walked out with stolen money from Anson's safe and he realized she was never coming home, he vowed he would be the only one to raise Heidi, that he would do everything to be the best father he could be. He hadn't realized just how hard it would be to hold down a career and earning a living while raising a child alone, but he was lucky to have his aunt on board to help every once in a while. He wouldn't have it any other way. They were content in their little world and he had grown used to being a single dad. It may have been tough sometimes, but he knew he was doing his absolute best, and Heidi was flourishing and becoming a wonderful human being.

He had just finished looking over some plans at one of his build sites out on a new neighborhood of tourist cabins at the base of the mountain when his cell phone started ringing. He passed the blueprints back to the contractor and pulled it out of his back pocket to see a random number calling him. He raised it to his ear and spoke.

"Hello?" he said as he stepped away from the group of builders who were all busy chatting and shouting instructions to one another.

"Hi... Anson?" the little voice came from the other end of the line and he covered his other ear so he could hear her better.

"Yeah?" he said as he stepped into the trees and into the quiet.

"Hi, sorry to bother you, it's Krystal from Beau's shop..."

The moment her voice hit him again he felt himself stiffen up and his skin burned with heat.

"Hi," he said, and his heart began to pound.

He dug his boot into the trunk of the nearest tree and tried not to let himself turn into a mess of confusion again.

"I was just letting you know that my aunt got back in touch and we have your rent money. It's here if you want to come get it? Or I can bring it to you?"

He looked out at the scene in front of him, at the group of men laughing and joking, getting ready to start a day's work while he was only going to be standing around like a spare part. He easily could have left them to their own devices, but he wasn't giving in that easily.

"I can collect it, but not until later," he found himself saying sternly. "What time do you close?"

"Not until 5pm," she said.

"Okay, I'll see you before then," he said and ended the call.

He put the phone into his back pocket and kicked the trunk of the tree again and scowled.

"What the fuck is wrong with you?" he said to himself and then shook his head and headed toward his truck.

This girl had seriously messed with his head.

HEIDI SKIPPED OUT OF THE SCHOOL GATES AS IT HIT HALF PAST three and Anson was there waiting for her. She looked just as sparkling as she had that morning and she was excited to see her dad and tell him all about her day. He loved collecting her from school. It was adorable to see her with her little friends and the way they all interacted with each other. The five years since she had come along had gone so fast and she already seemed so mature and well on her way to being a full-blown grown up. She chattered along about her lunch, how she had spent recess playing in the school yard collecting leaves with her two best friends, and then she had spent the afternoon learning poetry and had even written a few verses herself.

"I'll show you when we get home," she said proudly. "I've written them in my book."

"Awesome," Anson beamed as he looked down at her. "I can't wait to read them."

"It's about a cat," she told him matter-of-factly. "A big fluffy cat with long whiskers."

Anson smiled. Heidi loved cats. In fact, she loved all animals. Being from a shifter family, that was hardly surprising, but Heidi didn't have any powers of her own when it came to that kind of thing, and for once Anson was actually glad of it, especially with all the strange happenings that were going on around town.

He pulled down Main Street and Heidi bopped along to the music in the back seat.

"Can we get ice cream?" she said.

He looked at her in the rearview mirror and laughed. She was always wanting ice cream, and who could blame her?

"Well, I've got to go do a little bit of work first, sweetheart," he said. "But after, sure, why not."

"Yayyyy!" Heidi said as she bounced up and down and clapped her hands together. "I'm going to get strawberry and sprinkles."

"Fantastic idea," Anson said as he pulled the truck up against the curb and turned off the engine.

"Where are we going?" Heidi asked as she unclipped her belt.

"Just into this store," he said as he looked over his shoulder and smiled. "Come on."

When he had gotten Heidi out of the back seat and they were walking toward the paranormal store he felt his heart pick up pace. He was on full alert, the animal inside him was growling and growing fiercer, and he couldn't subdue it. He held Heidi's hand as he walked forward and with each step closer to the shop he caught scent of the incense but then also something lingering beneath it.

The scent that was driving him wild.

It was her.

Krystal.

He felt his whole body react, his skin prickled with heat and he felt wired and alert. He pushed it down as much as he could, guiding his daughter through the shop doorway ahead of him before he finally looked up and saw her standing there.

God fucking damn, she was beautiful.

Krystal turned and her long, wavy black hair flicked over one shoulder as she smiled, and her blue eyes glistened. Anson felt rooted to the spot, and Heidi let go of his hand and skipped into the store making "Oooh" and "Ahhh" noises at all the knickknacks and cool little trinkets that were for sale. She made a beeline for the glittering crystals and all the wonderful colors and Anson looked back to Krystal, who was watching with a warm smile on her face.

He finally let his shoulders relax, and something in him became calm. Heidi bounced around the store and was rabbiting away, chatting to Krystal, who was laughing and stepping forward, showing the little girl the different types of stone, from Tiger's Eye to Onyx, to Rose Quartz and Aventurine.

"I like this one," Heidi said, breaking Anson's daze.

She was holding a blue colored crystal and she twirled it around in her fingers.

"Well, I'm still learning," Krystal said. "But I think that's a Sodalite... it should help you with your creativity... So if you're painting today or doing any drawing, then it will help you do your very best!" she smiled widely and Heidi's eyes seemed to pop out of her head with adoration.

"Really?" she said with a beaming smile. "I've just been telling my daddy about my poems. I've been writing them today!"

Krystal's gaze traveled up to Anson and he felt his heart

click. This time, he felt a wave of calm, like she was settling the stormy sea inside him and being there with her and Heidi was bringing him a new level of peace.

"Wow, really?" Krystal asked.

Her gaze was on him and she was warmer with him too. As if the animosity that may have been there before, or, more likely, the awkwardness between them, had vanished. Heidi had cleared the path and brought them closer together just by being in the same room.

"Well, you better take it, then," Krystal said. "I mean, I owe your dad, anyway," she winked, and Anson couldn't help but smile.

"Can I have it please Daddy?" Heidi asked.

"Sure, of course you can," Anson said as he stepped further into the shop and rested his big, rough mountain man's hand down on the counter. "But let's pay for it, deal?"

He locked eyes with Krystal, and she smiled.

"Really, I feel bad you were kept waiting, as does my aunt…" she tried to protest.

Anson held up his hand and smiled warmly. He didn't want her to think he was such a complete jerk.

"Honestly, it's no problem. Your aunt is one of my best tenants."

She smiled and nodded meekly and then she reached down for the envelope on the side and passed it to him.

"Sorry again that it was late," she said.

Anson took it from her and smiled.

"Like I said, it's no problem," he said. "How's your aunt's trip?"

"All going well, from what I've heard," Krystal replied. "She called me this morning and said she'll check in again soon."

"And you're doing okay here holding down the fort?" he asked with a grin.

"Just about," Krystal laughed.

"Well, if you've got any trouble or need advice on anything regarding the building, don't hesitate to let me know."

"Thank you," she smiled.

Anson held the envelope and reached into his wallet to pull out some money for the crystal Heidi was jumping around and holding in her hand tightly like it was the most precious thing on Earth.

"Here," he said. "And thanks again."

Krystal watched as he made his way toward the door, but Heidi seemed reluctant to leave.

"Do you like ice cream?" she said suddenly to Krystal, who was already tidying away what looked like a recent delivery.

"Me?" she asked as she stopped what she was doing. "Well, sure, I love ice cream."

"Me and my dad are going for some, why don't you come with us?"

Anson felt his eyes widen. He had no idea where this had come from, but Heidi was clearly already completely taken with the cool girl in the paranormal shop who had given her a crystal and been kind to her.

Krystal smiled and he found that he was doing the same.

"That is so kind," Krystal said. "But I don't finish work for at least another hour. But you have a wonderful time and make sure you come back to see me soon, okay?"

"Okay," Heidi beamed. "I'll come back and show you all my drawings and poems I've done thanks to this new crystal!"

"That would be fantastic," Krystal smiled.

Anson waved his hand and said goodbye, and then he stepped outside the shop with his daughter who seemed happier and more excited than he had seen her in a long time.

"I love her," Heidi declared as they wandered into the ice cream parlor. "Did you see her hair? It was beautiful, like Snow White's, but loads longer."

Anson laughed.

"And that shop is so cool, I want to go back," Heidi said as she sat down in one of the candy pink booths that lined the walls. "I like her daddy. I think she and I will be friends."

He hadn't seen her so enamored with someone after one brief meeting before in her entire life, and it certainly was giving him some food for thought.

It appeared Krystal's arrival in town wasn't just having a strange effect on him. Now, his little girl was happy to have met her too… and he knew now that his world was about to be turned upside down.

CHAPTER 7

As the week drew to a close, Krystal was pleased with herself and all she had managed to accomplish within the store. She had dedicated her entire time while she had been there to unpacking and getting herself familiar with the place. She wanted to do the best job she could, and she wanted to invest herself in it fully so Beau could see her dedication when she came back from her travels.

She had wondered several times how her aunt was doing while she was away, and if she had managed to track down her mysterious friend and explain to him what had been happening back in Bridge Hollow, but she had yet to receive more than a few texts since the phone call about the safe. At least she knew she was okay, but she did wonder what she was up to, and if they had come up with any theories about the strange phenomena of the town.

It was Friday night and from up in the apartment Krystal could hear the town coming alive. She had been so worn out and tired once she had finished work every day that she had yet to venture out on an evening and see what Bridge Hollow was about. She didn't remember that side of things from when she was younger; in fact, she didn't even really remember Main Street, but as she had been walking around during the day she had seen a couple of places that looked like they showed promise where a social scene was concerned and as she looked across at the television she sighed and turned it off.

"I'm not staying in on a Friday night," she said to herself as she rose to her feet.

She stretched and wandered through to her bedroom, flicking through her closet and humming and harring over which outfit to wear. For her first night out in a small mountain town, she didn't want to go too overboard, but at the same time, she didn't want to be a wallflower, that had never been her style.

She pinned her long hair into big, round curlers on top of her head and left them there while she danced around her bedroom, lifting out skirts and jeans from the closet and holding them up against herself in the mirror. She chose a pair of black skinny jeans and a red camisole. To match, she slicked a deep red over her lips and winged her eyeliner, and when she was finished and let the rollers out of her hair, she grinned at herself in the mirror. She looked a million dollars, and for the first time in what could have been a year, she felt really happy with how she looked.

Back in the city she had always felt as if she were being judged, and it really seemed to bother her, but here, she simply didn't care. She didn't know anyone, and she didn't care what anyone thought of her. She was glad to be there and to mixing in the scene with the mountain folk for a change rather than the pretentious city boys who only wanted to talk about money and cars.

She grabbed her purse and her shearling jacket, pulled it on over her shoulders and let her hair tumble down her back, in thick, shiny waves. As she headed out the door, she smiled to herself and felt empowered. She had confidence in Bridge Hollow, she had sass and she wasn't afraid to be herself… and he felt really fucking good! She couldn't wait to get out on Main Street and have herself a fun time.

She wandered down and checked out the bars on either side of the street. Some of them looked a lot more subdued than the others, and some were clearly more bistros and wine bars, serving tapas and mainly catering to quiet diners and couples. It had been a long while since Krystal had hit a bar, and she fancied seeing what kind of wild side Bridge Hollow had to offer, even though she couldn't imagine it was anything too out there.

Her eyes flitted over the big statue of the man turning into the bear in the center of town and she couldn't help but smirk. There was so much power in the eyes, the bear looked as if it were bursting free of the man's skin and it made her own skin tingle. Her mind immediately traveled to Anson and she wondered if that was what happened to him… she still hadn't had it confirmed, but she was pretty sure he had to a be a shifter. But she had seen such a different side to him when he had entered the store to collect the rent money a few days earlier. He had brought an adorable little girl with him, with which Krystal had felt an immediate connection. Heidi had been like a light shining through all the darkness that seemed to be plaguing Bridge Hollow lately, and it was a good feeling to see a man like him being such an amazing father.

Krystal had never had a father of her own, and it always warmed her heart when she saw a man stepping up the challenge and being the best dad he could be. Anson clearly was doing just that, and it had made her like him even more, even if she was still trying to convince herself she didn't like him at all.

She continued walking and it wasn't long before she saw a bustling place with a crowd of people outside on the street. She noticed some of them were bikers, all clad in leather with big silver rings on their knuckles and sat astride Harley's. She was so used to hanging around in cocktail bars and attending corporate events, that being in this kind of environment was thrilling, and she felt herself drawn to it in an intense way. She was so busy keeping her eyes fixed on the door of the bar and the thumping music coming from inside, that she didn't notice the sign above her on the way in. She didn't notice the fact that she was walking right into a place called SHIFTERS BLISS.

Her eyes lit up as she stepped into the hot and steamy atmosphere of the bar. It was wilder in there than she had expected it to be, and it was clear that Bridge Hollow certainly knew how to handle Friday nights. The place was packed, the scent of booze and smoke was heavy in the air and it was hot and sweaty, making her pull her jacket off her shoulders straight away. She moved through the crowd and headed for the long wooden bar in the center of the room, where plenty of people were waiting to get served, but she saw the perfect spot right at the end with a free stool waiting for her to slip into. At the back of the room a huge stage was set, and a band was playing. The music was loud and heavy, but it seemed to work and there were plenty of people dancing in front of them and throwing themselves into the mix.

Krystal reached the bar and she climbed onto the stool and got herself comfortable. She was lucky to have found it, the place was so rammed she couldn't believe that one was even available. She looked at all the people who were in the bar with her and she could tell some of them had to be residents of Bridge Hollow, but some of them could have easily been tourists too. She wondered if that was how she appeared, she had hidden herself away on an evening so well she didn't think anyone in town would know who she was and they would probably think she was some kind of paranormal nut coming to geek up on the weird happenings.

She was aware of some of the bikers heading into the bar and the way they got served straight away. They downed bottles of beer with whiskey chasers, and then they all took a booth on the outside of the room.

"Hey there," a girl's voice cut in over the loud thump of the music and it made Krystal draw her eyes back to the bar.

It was one of the servers, a cherubic looking blonde girl who was smiling from ear to ear.

"Can I get you something to drink?" she asked as she wiped down the countertop with one of her bar mops.

"Yes, please," Krystal called back to her. The girl couldn't have been much older than her, maybe she was even younger. Krystal had never been very good at guessing people's ages, but it was clear that they were both in their twenties and she could imagine becoming friends with someone like her. A girl who worked in the hottest bar in town would have to have a bit about them, and she could imagine her being the closest thing to a city girl that she would find around these parts.

Krystal scanned the refrigerators along the back of the bar and up to the spirits held in place by optics. She wasn't much of a drinker; in fact, she didn't like the taste of alcohol that much at all, but she felt the need to take the edge off her nerves of being there alone, and she had the feeling there wouldn't be any kind of cocktail menu she could browse.

"You need a suggestion?" the girl asked with her head cocked to the side.

"Yeah," Krystal admitted with a half laugh. "Something that doesn't taste like alcohol…"

The girl laughed and turned around to grab a glass.

"Vodka and lime," she said with a wink as she cracked some ice into the glass, poured some vodka into it from one of the upturned bottles on the wall and then topped it up with soda water and a big squeeze of fresh lime.

She handed it to Krystal, and she smiled, it looked just like lemonade so she may as well give it a shot. She took a sip and was pleasantly surprised.

"Mmm," she said. "That's perfect. But don't give me too many, okay?"

The girl laughed and nodded.

"I'm Wendy," she said as she held out her hand. "Are you on vacation?"

Krystal shook her head as she took another sip.

"Nope, I just moved here," she said with a grin.

"You've moved here?" asked Wendy with a raised brow. "Like temporarily, for a project or something?"

Krystal shook her head.

"No one just moves to Bridge Hollow…" Wendy laughed. "This is the kind of place people visit, or they come to write the great novel they've always dreamed of, but end up leaving after a month… In fact, we had a girl who did just that a couple months ago and she never left. She's still living here with her man and loving it."

"I'm here for good too… Hopefully," Krystal said.

Wendy nodded and smiled.

"Interesting," she said.

"I'm Krystal," Krystal held out her hand the two shook. "My aunt runs the paranormal store on Main Street and I'm helping her out while she's away for a few weeks."

"Oh, so you're Beau's niece!" Wendy's face cracked into a big welcoming smile of recognition.

"The very same," she laughed.

"Oh, I've heard a lot about you," Wendy grinned. "Your aunt is an absolute gem; we all love her around here."

Wendy had such a genuinely nice and welcoming vibe that Krystal was very glad to have met her. She could see herself sitting up at the bar and making friends with her, she seemed like the kind of girl she would have a lot in common with.

A group of rowdy tourists started to holler at Wendy for drinks and she rolled her eyes with a smile at Krystal before she moved on down the bar and started to serve them. Krystal laughed, she was already having a great time and she couldn't believe she had let herself sit in the apartment for the past week basically living like a hermit. She may have needed the rest, but she easily could have been missing out on so much fun!

The band finished up their song, and the crowd whooped and cheered before the singer started to talk to the room. He started to amp them up for the next song, acting as if he was on stage in a huge stadium in front of thousands of screaming fans, rather than on a small stage in this small-town bar. Krystal couldn't help but laugh.

She felt an arm brush against hers and her skin instantly tingled. She glanced over and noticed a muscular physique next to her and it made her heart clatter in her chest. He looked down at her with his big, brown eyes and a smirk flitted across his lips.

"What's so funny?" he asked her.

He had clearly been watching her for a while and had seen her smiling at the band.

Anson.

Here he was, and this time, he was certainly much different than he had been the first time they had met.

She sat up straight on the stool and cocked her head to the side.

"I was just wondering if it's this exciting for the band playing on a stage this small, imagine what it would be like in front of thousands."

Anson nodded and leaned in to let someone closer to the bar behind him.

"Philosophical," he grinned.

She rolled her eyes with a smirk and shrugged.

"So, you finally left the witch cave?" Anson teased. "How are things going over at the store?"

"Witch cave?" she laughed. "Great, now I know what you really think!"

He laughed.

"Yeah, it's all going well," she continued. "I'd say I'm a pro already in all things mystical."

"You certainly made quite the impression on Heidi," Anson said, and his eyes were looking down on her, glistening with warmth.

"She's wonderful," Krystal admitted.

It felt good to be close to him, and this time, she felt his energy so intensely it was as if she were drawn to him in an even more feverish way. He was so big and tall and so handsome, his stubble and beard only added to his ruggedness and it was turning her on.

No clean-cut pretty city boys here.

Anson was all man.

She smiled coyly and sipped her drink. After the way they had met, they were certainly warming up to each other.

She could feel he hadn't taken his eyes off her.

"Have you been waiting for me to come in here?" she asked with a raised brow.

Anson threw his head back and laughed.

"I don't come in here myself," he said. "But I did notice you haven't been around town much…"

"Well, if you don't come in here, then why are you in here right now?" she grinned.

"Debt collecting," he winked.

"Your specialty," Krystal mused.

"Not really," he said. "I'm just following up something from one of my brothers for another property. He owns this place."

She watched as he looked across the bar and he raised his head and nodded at someone on the other side. Krystal tried to follow his gaze and see where he was looking, but it was so crowded in there she must have missed their exchange.

"Well, I'm only down here because I couldn't face another night locked away in the apartment," she said. "I've been working so hard I figured I deserved a night off."

"Good for you," he smiled.

She sipped her drink and turned away slightly. She still couldn't exactly figure him out. Had he come over to talk to her? Or was he just waiting for someone?

She looked back to him and he was staring down at her with intense eyes. The heat between them was growing, and as someone moved past him and pushed him slightly, they bumped up against each other and it made her gasp. Her whole body reacted to him and it was unnerving.

There was something very, very deep and sensual about Anson. And he was directing it on her, but she could also tell he was holding himself back.

"If you need anything," he said as he stepped back from her and the force that seemed to be pulling them together faded. "Just call me, okay? It's an old building… things can easily go wrong."

She nodded and she felt disappointed that he was no longer right up against her. She had liked feeling him close, and she couldn't pull herself away from his eyes, they were so enchanting.

"I will," she managed to whisper.

He went to move away and then he turned back and looked at her again. He was clearly conflicted about something and she was beginning to feel driven wild with impatience. If she had been back home in the city and had met someone like this in a bar, she wouldn't have felt so cautious and nervous. But there was something about Anson that made her nervous in such a good way that she was worried about making the wrong move and messing it all up.

"I'll call by tomorrow," he said as if he had changed his mind about letting her have the option to call him. "See how you're doing…"

He smiled and Krystal bit her bottom lip.

She could see he didn't want to leave her there, but there was something pulling him away.

"I have to go," he said. "My daughter…"

Of course. It was getting late, and he likely had a sitter to get back to.

"Sure," she smiled. "Say hi to her for me."

Anson nodded and started to back away, his eyes never leaving hers and her heart still raging away below the surface of her skin.

Whatever was happening between them was completely new to her, it was something raw and powerful.

And it was exciting as hell.

CHAPTER 8

She spent the whole night tossing and turning, her body burning hot and her pussy aching. Since she met Anson, she had been constantly turned on, and the second she thought about him her skin seemed to shudder.

Now that she had seen him again in the bar, she knew for certain that she wanted him. She had been trying to fight it, but there was something so amazing about the way they had connected. It didn't need to be said, it just existed between them heavily and unignorable.

It was a chemistry like she had never thought possible, and now, she was feeling addicted to it, as if she needed her fix or she would be doomed.

When her alarm finally sounded the following morning, she was exhausted, and she dragged herself out of bed and into the shower knowing she was likely going to have a busy day ahead of her. It was Saturday, an always busy day in Bridge Hollow. With it being the run-up to Halloween, she had seen that the town was already decorating to pull in tourists, and she could imagine that folks from not so far away would likely take day trips there. Surely, they would want some kind of mystical souvenir from the paranormal store, and she was going to be hectic and rushed. But she also knew there was a possibility of Anson coming to see her if he stuck to his word, which kept her going and gave her a definite spring in her step.

She got ready quickly and drank two cups of coffee while she dried her hair and applied her makeup. She chose a simple outfit for the day, wanting to remain as aloof as possible while also pulling off effortlessly sexy. She chose a pair of tight indigo skinny jeans, some flat pumps and a white tight sweater cut in a low V neck. She left her face bare, only using a tiny bit of lip-gloss, mascara and a rosy cheek of blusher, before she put in a pair of small stud earrings and a spritz of perfume.

She felt amazing, and yet she had gone quite simple.

"Sometimes, simple is best," she said aloud to herself as she grabbed her keys and her cell phone and headed out the door.

When she opened the hallway to the back of the store and stepped inside the gorgeous smell of incense hit her immediately and she couldn't help but smile. She truly did love it here, this place felt as if it spoke to her soul.

She turned on the fairy lights on the beams, began to light the candles, set some atmospheric music playing and opened the front doors before she took out the table and chairs and started to set them up with their usual wares.

Once she was back inside it wasn't even 9am, but she was wide awake and raring to go. She had been spending a lot of her time while the store had been quiet on studying the subjects on the shelves, both via the books that Beau kept in there, and by browsing online.

She had learned a lot about tarot, she had been holding

and cleansing crystals, learning their properties and letting herself be drawn to some of her own. She had found herself cradling a rose quartz in her palm, and when she had learned all that it signified and could bring to the owner, she thought it was very apt. The stone of love and attraction. She had read tips online that after they had been cleansed, they should be carried by the owner at all times, so she slipped it into the back pocket of her jeans and hoped it would bring her good fortune when it came to Anson.

A customer wandered in the doorway and she smiled and wished them a good morning. She could tell that they were from out of town and they were a young couple quietly discussing the theories that were surrounding Bridge Hollow. Krystal listened as best she could.

"I mean at the beginning of the year those two men went missing," the guy said. "I just think it's weird that nothing has been found out by now... Do you think they were murdered?"

Krystal felt a shiver roll over her. She had heard the news about two hunters going missing, and she had discussed it with her aunt, but it had been something that had made a lot of people of the town clam up. No one wanted to discuss the fact that two of their own had disappeared. It was too frightening for any of them to comprehend and no one knew the truth.

"I don't know," the girl said. "But I've always loved visiting this town at this time of year. It gives me the creeps."

Krystal was aware of them turning and glancing at her and she lifted her head and smiled.

"Is there anything I can help you with?" she asked as the girl slowly approached the desk.

"This place has moved, right?" the girl asked.

Krystal nodded.

"I thought it looked different," she said. "It's been a while since I've been back. I like visiting before the craziness of the yearly festival."

Krystal had heard a lot about this festival, and she was excited to experience it in a month's time.

"Are you from close by?" she asked.

"A couple of hours drive," the girl smiled. "I think the last time I came into the store the lady gave me a tarot reading, is she here?"

"Oh, I'm sorry, that's my aunt and she's away traveling at the moment," Krystal said.

"Oh, that's a shame," the girl nodded as she picked up a hand poured candle and placed it on the counter to buy. "I love getting my fortune told."

Krystal smiled. It looked like she was going to have to learn and hoped that she had the same gifts as her aunt.

The couple paid and left the shop and it got Krystal to thinking about doing a little tarot reading of her own. Maybe she could look into the future and discover something not just about herself, but the future of the town too and what her place would be there.

She was lost in a colorful world of thoughts when there was a light rap at the door, and she looked up to see Anson standing in the doorway. He was so big his body nearly eclipsed the entire frame and his big arms were bare and showing off his incredible tan and muscles.

She swallowed and felt her jaw sag open a little.

He looked so good.

So good, it was making her pussy throb all over again.

He smiled at her and the light from the sun caught his eyes and she was sure she saw them glisten with a golden amber that she had never seen in them before.

"Morning," he said with a wry smile.

He could clearly see the effect he was having on her and he liked it too.

"Morning," she said breathlessly as she flipped her hair over her shoulder and tried not to crumple to the floor in a mess of desire.

He stepped inside and she couldn't take her eyes off him. He was wearing low slung jeans and she could see a jut of muscle running into the waistband. It made her heart dance and she had to pull her eyes away, not wanting to look like she was undressing him right there and then in her mind. His shirt was tight and rolled up to the elbows, and his big, rough hands looked well-worn as if he had been working outside.

"So, you came by…" she said mischievously as he approached the counter.

He nodded and looked down at her. She felt so tiny next to him, she could only imagine the strength he must have inside him.

"I said I would," he smiled.

"Where's Heidi?" she asked. "No big plans on this lovely Saturday?"

"Actually, we have big, big plans," he laughed. "She's currently with my aunt, but later today I have been roped into making Halloween decorations." He raised his eyebrows and Krystal couldn't help but laugh.

"I can imagine you being very crafty," she teased. "Apron, glue gun, lace and ribbons…"

"Exactly," he said sternly. "And I take my art very seriously."

His face cracked into a warm smile and Krystal started to laugh. He was funny. Who would have known after the first time they had met, and he had been so strange?

"Well, that sounds like a lovely afternoon," she said. "It must be so much fun with her, she's great."

"She really is," he agreed. "My little sidekick and constant pain in my ass, but I love her more than anything."

Krystal's heart ached.

What a man.

She smiled.

"I was actually wondering if there was any chance you could help us… I know you're working here today and you're probably going to be busy, but Heidi has talked nonstop about the girl in the paranormal shop since the moment she met you. And she wants some more crystals."

Her whole soul felt like it was lighting up, but she tried to hold it together.

"Of course," she said. "That would be great."

She looked around the shop and saw all the work she had to do, and she didn't want to turn him down, but knew there was no way she was going to get away during the shop's opening hours.

"I don't close until 5pm," she said.

"That's fine," he smiled. "Why don't we pick you up at closing?"

She could barely believe what was happening.

"Okay," she grinned. "That would work."

He turned and began walking toward the door and then looked back at her.

"See you later Krystal," he said before he slipped out and back on Main Street.

Her head was swimming and her heart was thumping so loud she could hear the rush of blood in her ears.

Anson had come looking for her and asked her to go and hang out with him and his daughter.

This was absolutely insane and literally the best thing that could have happened to her. She didn't know what had changed, but she loved the fact that it had. And now she had plans to see him later and she had never been more excited.

She reached into her back pocket to feel the rose quartz. It was red hot and full of energy and hope, just like she was.

"Thank you, little stone," she smiled.

She was beginning to love this magical place and all that came with it, and she was certainly turning into a believer.

CHAPTER 9

*A*nson sat at the island in the center of his kitchen and looked out of the window thoughtfully to the view of the mountains. He had had quite a week, and he still didn't quite know what to make of it all.

He was lucky that he had his Aunt Nora close and that he could ask her for advice when it came to these kinds of things, but he had to admit it had felt strange opening up the way he had.

When he hadn't been able to shake Krystal from his thoughts and his body had been wired for days, wanting to hunt for her and find her, he had told his aunt everything and asked for her help.

"You know what this is don't you?" she had told him.

He nodded his head slowly, even though he was scared to admit it.

"This is the one you've been waiting for Anson," she had said. "This girl, whoever she is, her soul is the one yours has been searching for your whole life. The stars have aligned, and you have been brought together."

He had nodded and held his head in his hands.

He didn't know if he was ready for this, but it didn't seem like he could fight it.

"I always said it would just be Heidi and I," he had told his aunt. "I have never wanted to be involved with another woman after what happened… it was too painful."

Aunt Nora had wrapped a loving arm around his shoulder.

"You can't live your life pushing against what is meant to be," she had told him. "Your kind isn't meant to be alone, Anson. They have a fated mate out there and when you meet them, nothing else is ever the same again."

He had never really believed in the concept before. He thought he had found the love of his life when he had met Heidi's mother, but she had turned out to be just a phase. The way he felt about Krystal was like an unexpected bolt of lightning. Like his whole body had been shocked into noticing her. He was drawn to her like he had never been drawn to anything. He could sense her before he saw her, he could smell her scent in the air, and it drove him wild. He had heard some of his pack brothers talk about this kind of thing, but he had never really been sure that it existed. And now here he was, experiencing it for real and unable to think about anything else.

"She's consuming me," he had told his aunt. "And I barely even know her."

"Your souls already know one another's," Aunt Nora had smiled knowingly. "And when you imprint on her you will understand."

Anson had always been afraid of this, but now he had met Krystal he wasn't anymore. Suddenly, things just made sense.

"And Heidi loved her immediately," he had laughed.

"Well, there you go," his aunt had beamed. "If you needed any more encouragement then, surely, it is that? But you can't fight fate Anson… if you do then it will drive you mad and you will spend your life miserable and troubled. You'll be in turmoil because your heart will be wanting something you've denied yourself unnecessarily."

He knew she was right.

He had spent that whole night awake thinking about Krystal. About what he was feeling and the fact that he had tried to push it down and ignore it, but it had just grown stronger. Now, he knew there was no way he could continue. He would drive himself mad, just like his aunt had told him, and he owed it to Heidi and to himself to let his fate pan out the way it was supposed to.

He had been alone for a long time, and his daughter deserved a mother. She had loved Krystal so much on sight that he knew it was the extra validation he needed before he embarked on this journey and let his heart open.

He had always told himself that no one would ever be good enough to come into Heidi's life. But maybe that was because he had always been waiting for this feeling, and now, he had found it.

HEIDI CAME BOUNCING INTO THE LIVING ROOM AND LUGGED with her a box full of colored cards, scissors, ribbons, stickers and dried fruit that Aunt Nora had helped her make months before.

"I want to make a garland for the door," she grinned. "Are we going to decorate the house?"

She clapped her hands together in excitement, and as Anson looked toward the clock and saw that it was approaching four thirty, he finally felt as if he could let Heidi in on his little secret that he knew was going to brighten her day.

"I've managed to get us a helper," he said with a wry smile. "I saw Krystal earlier."

Heidi's eyes widened and she grinned from ear to ear.

"Krystal from the shop?"

Anson nodded.

"I invited her to come over and help us make and put up the decorations, and she said she would love to."

"Oh my goodness!" Heidi shrieked. "Daddy, that is the best news ever!"

She ran toward him and threw herself into his arms. Anson kissed the top of her head and held her close. He loved seeing her so happy, it radiated out of her and went into him and it was such a wonderful feeling.

He had spent so long denying himself the right to love, that when it had found him, he had almost tried to push it away and forget it existed. But it had been Heidi, who had shown him the way. She had the intuition and the foresight that Krystal was someone meant to be with them, and he couldn't wait for them to all be together in the same room again.

He hugged her again and then whispered in her ear…

"And we're going to pick her up from the store, so come on, get your things."

Heidi jumped up and began to dance. Anson felt like the stars were aligning; his aunt was right.

A shifter's fate was impossible to ignore.

CHAPTER 10

Krystal had never been so glad to close the shop as she stood waiting by the doorway for the sight of Anson's truck. It had been a long, busy and enjoyable day, but since he had come to visit her, all she had been able to think about was locking the doors and heading off with him to spend the evening.

Her nerves were starting to fizzle to the surface, and she took a few deep breaths to calm herself. She didn't want to psyche herself out before he had even arrived, but she was finding it difficult not to overthink with each passing second.

The candles had been blown out and the shop was dark. The dusk was already rolling in and some of the taverns had opened along Main Street, with early bird drinkers and diners already filling up the tables inside.

When she saw a set of headlights come closer, she knew it was him. They slowed and the truck stopped, and she ran her hands through her hair to bounce up the curls. She stepped outside and locked the store door behind her.

It was such a strange feeling to her that she couldn't see him, yet she knew it was Anson.

She felt him.

She felt his eyes on her and she felt his presence. It was already carved into her and she felt bonded and chosen, as if they would never truly be apart again.

She had heard of this kind of thing. Her mother had warned her about it when she had been a teenager. She had told her about the power a shifter man could have when it came to claiming his woman, and that she had to watch for the signs.

Krystal had thought she had it all figured out, but since she had met Anson, all the things she had been told in the past had gone out the window. He was something she hadn't been expecting, and now that he had arrived in her life, she needed to explore it.

"Hi," he smiled as he stepped out of the driver's door and made his way around to greet her.

He looked down at her and reached for the passenger door, opening it wide and letting her climb in.

"Thank you," Krystal said as she pulled herself up and inside and then was instantly grabbed and smothered with hugs by Heidi.

"Krystal!" Heidi called. "I am so glad you're coming to help us. Daddy said you're going to show us how to make garlands."

Anson climbed back in the driver's side and laughed before he shrugged and seemed to agree with the suggestion.

"Did he now...?" Krystal teased.

"We have everything ready," Heidi continued. "I got all my craft boxes down from the spare room."

She was bubbling with excitement and it was catching. Krystal's nerves had completely disappeared now she was with them both and all she could focus on was how easy and chilled things were. Their energies all mixed so well together, as if they had known each other for a lifetime.

Anson drove the mountain roads and left the main part of town. He headed out toward one of the quieter neighborhoods with bigger houses, and Krystal was in awe of how stunning they all were.

"Wow," she said. "These are amazing cabins."

Anson smiled and nodded.

"I built most of them," he said as he looked at her. "My company did anyway. We own a lot of the land around town with my family being one of the original settlers here."

"Wow, really?"

He nodded.

"So, around eight years ago, when I was just starting to get good at this building thing, I thought, *Why don't we cater for some of the rich crazies who like to come out to this neck of the woods?* I mean, people have lake houses and vacation homes all over the country. Why not here?"

He was confident and intelligent, and it was even more of a turn on. When she had initially met him, he had come across as such a brutish jerk, but now she was getting to know him she could see how wonderful he truly was.

"So, I set the wheels in motion and we started with six executive cabins… now we have ten. And ours is right at the top of the neighborhood."

The cabins were more than that… they looked like wood and glass mansions nestled discreetly in amongst the trees. Anson weaved the truck in and around the road easily, his hands moving at exactly the right time as if he knew each bend by heart.

He slowed and pulled up in front of one of the smaller cabins out of the ten that they had seen, but it was still incredible. It was traditional in style but with some modern features thrown in, and she could see that part of the roof at the back was glass and it looked as if it had been extended.

Heidi was chattering away in the back and she unclipped

her belt and opened the door, running toward the porch at full speed and beckoning Krystal to come with her.

She followed her and Anson closed the door after her before he locked the car and took the keys to the front door. He slipped them in and opened it wide and when she walked in behind Heidi, she instantly felt that this place was a warm and welcoming home. She had been in some amazing houses over the years, but they had been cold and clinical. This place was inviting and full of good energy, and she looked up to Anson and smiled at him with a blush.

They went through to the kitchen and living space and she loved how big and open plan it was. Heidi hadn't been exaggerating when she had said that she had brought down all her craft supplies, and there were three large Perspex boxes waiting for them on the island, filled to the brim with multicolored felt and ribbons, wire and sticks, fairy lights and patterns, wool and buttons.

"Well, look at all this," Krystal said. "What a collection."

Heidi beamed and sat and instantly started to open the boxes and pull things out and onto the countertop.

Anson was looking at Krystal and she turned to him and their eyes met. She felt a rush of longing throb right through her and she noticed that he was breathing fast too.

"Let me get you something," he said. "A drink?"

"Thank you," Krystal said. "I'll have whatever you're having."

Anson opened the refrigerator and brought out a bottle of red wine. He uncorked it effortlessly and poured her a glass. Krystal took it from him and smiled, and then she went to take a sip but had to pull away. There was no way she could drink it.

"Okay, I have a confession," she said.

Anson looked at her with worry, but she laughed and

shook her head to let him know it wasn't anything to be alarmed about.

"I don't like wine," she said, and she cringed as if she had just told him the worst thing in the world. "I'm sorry... In fact, I don't like alcohol that much in general."

Anson's brow unfurled and a look of relief flooded over him.

"You have no idea how happy that makes me to hear that," he said as he reached and took the glass away from her and threw the contents of it down the sink with a splash. "I don't drink either. Not at all. I've been teetotal for years."

"Really?" she asked. Completely dumbfounded as to how Anson could have gotten any more perfect than he already was.

"Yeah, it was never something I enjoyed," he said as he looked at Heidi, as if the reason was something to do with her being in his life. "And you know, I have my responsibilities..."

Krystal's heart was melting.

He was everything she had ever dreamed of. How could her mom have disliked guys like him? Maybe she had been brainwashed by her own parents and had just never had the chance to explore things herself and be proved wrong.

He laughed and rested the almost full wine bottle in the sink and then he went back to the refrigerator.

"Okay," he grinned. "Let's start again."

He brought out a bottle of lemonade and a smoothie that looked homemade, he had fresh juices and mineral waters, and he let Krystal take her pick.

"Oh, I'll have to try a mountain spring water," she said as she took the bottle from his hands. "Thank you."

He chose the same and they untwisted the caps from the tops of the bottles and then chinked them together before they drank. Their eyes never leaving each other's for a moment.

Krystal could have kept looking at him forever, but Heidi was already bouncing around on her chair and asking them to sit with her.

"Come on guys," she said with glee. "Let's make a wreath for the door with these dried pumpkins and lights... I have these leaves too."

Anson smiled, and so did Krystal.

Out of an initial meeting of what would officially go down as the worst in history, they had found something special here... and now, Krystal was relaxing in this wonderful home with a gorgeous little girl and her dad. Could this be the family-life she had missed and craved so much?

They started to unpack the lights and the faux autumn leaves, and Anson watched as the two girls got to work. There was a lot of crafts to be done, and they were eager to get going. Before the night was through, their cabin was going to be decked out for Halloween so well, people would be traveling to Bridge Hollow just to see it.

"She is honestly one of the most amazing kids I've ever met." Krystal smiled as she and Anson sat on the couch together later that evening.

Heidi had been exhausted by the time it had hit 9pm, and after being super excited about being able to stay up late, she had eventually crashed and gone to bed without having to be prompted.

"She is incredible," Anson said humbly.

"And you're the reason," Krystal continued. "You really are a fantastic father."

He shrugged and looked momentarily embarrassed.

"It's not always this easy," he admitted. "But I wouldn't change a thing. It's been the two of us for so long now... since the beginning really. We don't know it any other way."

Krystal wanted to ask what had happened to Heidi's mom, but she didn't want to overstep.

"Would you mind if I asked what happened... with her mom?" she asked tentatively and almost in a whisper.

Anson locked eyes with her and smiled before he looked away, as if he couldn't bear to admit it to another person.

"She was an addict," he said finally. "She left us when Heidi was only a few weeks old. She stole money from me and my business and one morning she was just gone... Five years later and we haven't heard a word from her. Not that I want to. Heidi is much better off without her in her life, but sometimes I can tell she misses the presence of a mother figure."

Krystal's heart was breaking for him, and she reached out and touched his arm. Her fingertips grazed his hot skin and the heat from within him made her gasp.

He looked at her and their eyes met again. There was something so deep and intense there, something made it impossible for her to break away.

"I know the truth about this place," she whispered. "I lived here myself when I was a child, and my mom and I left before I had a chance to figure things out... but she told me..."

Anson's eyes were on her, his pupils wide and engulfed with passion.

"I know about the shifters..." she let the statement hang in the air. "You are one, aren't you?"

Her heart was racing in her chest and she felt her palms go clammy. She wanted to know the truth about him, but at the same time, she was afraid. If he confirmed what she thought he was, then she was going to be conflicted. She didn't want to disrespect everything her mother had always told her, but she also knew how she felt. She was falling for this man. And it was impossible to stop. Something powerful had brought them together and they needed to explore their connection.

"Yes," he said, his eyes not leaving hers for a second. "I'm from the bear pack here. Does that frighten you?"

He said it so calmly, so honestly, that it was hard for her to feel any other way than a certain kind of relief.

"No," she smiled. "I thought it would… but it doesn't."

He smiled and took her hand.

"I always said I wouldn't get involved with anyone," he moved a little closer. "But the moment I saw you, something inside me came alive. And I can't ignore it."

"Me neither," she said in a whisper.

She squeezed his hand reassuringly and he lifted his other one to brush a loose strand of hair behind her ear. The sensation of his fingertips connecting with her skin made her bones tremble and her heart race. He was awakening things in her too… things she hadn't known before and things she was quickly becoming addicted too.

The tension between them was mounting, and Krystal knew she wanted to kiss him. She didn't truly know what the implications were, but the way she was feeling in this moment told her that she wanted to spend the rest of her life with this man. She never wanted them to be apart.

He leaned forward and their lips grazed against each other's.

"Do you know what happens when men like me find our one true mate?" he whispered.

Krystal nodded. Her mother had told her that once they had been connected, their souls would be entwined forever.

Everything in her head was telling her to run, but her heart was ruling and there was no stilling it.

"My mother told me… that you claim someone…"

Anson nodded.

Krystal swallowed nervously and looked up into his eyes.

"I can't fight this," she whispered.

The pull between them was so strong it was physically beginning to ache. She wanted him so badly, but she had to be sure.

"I can't kiss you," he said as he pulled away. "If I do… there is no going back."

Krystal looked away and breathed out deeply, her heart was pounding so hard and her mind was a mess. She felt so strongly toward him, but everything in her life up until this point had told her to run from men like him. How could she just go against all that without doing some serious soul searching?

"I should go," she said as she got to her feet and smoothed her hands down her jeans. "I know how I feel, but I'm so confused."

Anson nodded and put his head in his hands.

"Me too," he said. "It's been Heidi and I for such a long time…"

He looked up to her and smiled weakly. It was clear they were both conflicted, and yet their passion was so extraordinarily strong. Neither of them had ever felt anything like it before and it was knocking them both off their feet and moral compasses.

Krystal looked across at the carnage they had all left on the island in the kitchen and the table beside it. The leftovers of the Halloween crafts and the lovely little things they had made. It had been a wonderful evening, and now, she had had her suspicions confirmed. Anson was a shifter, and if she got involved with him, she would be with him for all time. Their souls would merge into one, she would be claimed by him and no one would ever be able to break them apart.

Fate had them in its sights.

"Thank you for tonight," she smiled as she grabbed her jacket and raced toward the door. "Don't worry about getting me home, I can walk."

"No!" he said as he rose to his feet. "You can't walk home; we are miles from Main Street."

She chewed her bottom lip and thought of the sleeping little girl in the bedroom down the hall and the way she had come here and fallen in fast. She didn't even want to go, but she knew she had to be strong and resist spending the actual night with him.

"I'll call a cab," she smiled.

"There aren't any around here at this time of night," he said as he looked up to the clock. "I'll wake Heidi and bring her with us."

"No," Krystal shook her head. "Please don't do that."

He smiled and shrugged.

"Then please, take the spare room?" he asked her. "I can drive you back first thing. As early as you want."

Krystal couldn't think of anything more perfect. Waking up in the same house as him and Heidi and seeing how they got to spend their morning.

"Okay," she smiled. "As long as it's no trouble."

"Trouble?" he asked with a raised brow. "There's no way I'm letting you out of here into the dark night alone. Come on, I'll show you the space."

They walked down the hallway hand in hand, and Krysta's heart was on fire. This had been the most perfect evening, and now, it didn't even have to end until the morning.

She rolled to her side and yawned. The warmth around her was lush and so soft she felt as if she were sleeping wrapped up in marshmallows. It had been the best night's sleep of her life, and when she opened her eyes, it took her a moment to figure out where she was.

The room wasn't the one at the apartment that she had been calling her own. But a stunningly modern one with a huge king-sized bed. She sat up and blinked in a daze and it came rushing back to her that she was at Anson's and Heidi's house. She pulled the covers up to her chin and grinned.

Last night had been so perfect.

They had had the most wonderful time and Anson had been nothing but the perfect gentlemen. He had asked her to spend the night in the guest room and had even resisted kissing her at the doorway before he went off to bed himself. But it had been hard for them both. Krystal hadn't known if she would have been able to do it, if the pull would have been too strong, but what kept her head fixed on her shoulders was the knowledge that she had to speak with her aunt. She had to know the reason why her mother had felt the way she did. She had spent her whole life believing these men to be bad. Was there something she was missing? How could Anson be so perfect, how could she feel so pulled to him, if he was really such a bad guy?

She knew deep within her heart that he wasn't. But she also needed some answers. She needed to know she wasn't about to make the biggest mistake of her life. Even if her soul wanted it more than anything.

She rose to her feet and looked in the mirror. She had slept so soundly she can't have moved in the night at all, as her hair still fell around her face in soft waves and she didn't look disheveled one bit.

She took a sip of water from the glass on the nightstand, and then she went into the adjoining bathroom and quickly washed her face in the sink and freshened up a little before she headed toward the door.

When she stepped out into the hallway, she could smell the delicious scent of bacon and her stomach actually growled. They had eaten the night before, but since she had come to town, it was almost as if she had forgotten about food, she had been so wrapped up in everything else...

The legends...

The store...

The hot as hell shifter man who had completely turned her head!

She stepped lightly down the hallway and her insides were warm and full of anticipation. When she turned the corner and moved into the kitchen and living space it was amazing to see Anson and Heidi up at the kitchen counter cooking together, with a large pot of coffee freshly brewed and waiting.

Heidi was sitting up on the counter, watching the bacon sizzle in the pan as Anson sliced fresh bread and lay it out in a basket.

"Wow," Krystal laughed as she moved toward them. "Would you look at this!"

"Krystal!" Heidi bounced down from the counter and ran across to her. She wrapped her arms around her legs and her waist and hugged her tight.

Anson smiled over at them both, and she could see the happiness in his eyes. As far as morning welcomes went, this was topping the list as her all-time favorite.

He moved toward the coffee and picked up the pot to pour her a mug. Krystal and Heidi joined him over at the counter and she leaned against it and cradled the cup in her hands.

"I could get used to this," Krystal teased. "Do you do this every morning?"

Anson nodded.

"We cook on the weekends," he smiled, his eyes catching hers as he worked away slicing the loaf of bread. "On weekdays, it's usually cereals, fruits and oatmeal."

He winked and Krystal bit her bottom lip to hide the fact she was smiling from ear to ear. She felt so happy and content there with them, it actually already felt like home.

"Daddy is an amazing cook," Heidi beamed as she started to carry an unopened carton of orange juice to the breakfast table. "And he makes mean pancakes."

Anson and Krystal both laughed.

"That's right, but for now you're both just going to have to settle for my mediocre bacon sandwiches… I hope they won't be too much of a disappointment," he teased with a wink.

"Well, it all smells amazing," Krystal said as she wandered across to help Heidi pour the juice into the three glasses that were arranged around the table at each place setting. "In fact, I can already tell it's going to be the best meal I've had since I came to town."

Heidi clapped her hands together and the two girls sat as Anson kept working away in the kitchen. He brought the basket of bread over to the table, followed by the coffee and some fresh butter, and last but not least, the bacon.

They all sat together and made their own sandwiches, with Krystal stepping in to help Heidi when she asked for it. Everything felt so easy and natural, as if it had always been this way. It was crazy to think that only two weeks before she had never met either of them before.

"Is the store open today?" Anson asked as he sipped his coffee.

Krystal couldn't take her eyes off his big hands and wondered what they would look like when they turned into paws. Big bear paws that could tear a grown man to shreds.

"Later on, for a few hours," she smiled. "If it wasn't October and getting so close to this big festival that everyone talks about then I probably wouldn't... but my aunt says these are the busiest months and the tourists like to shop on Sunday's so..."

"That they do," he raised his eyebrows. "You should see town on a Sunday night, it's not much quieter than a Friday."

"It must be fun," she said. "In the city, there was always somewhere to be and somewhere to go, but it felt so lonely. Here, it is so much smaller and intimate, but it feels more exciting. And I haven't felt lonely here once, isn't that strange?"

Anson was watching her speak with kind eyes and she caught him smiling at her.

"It's the little things," he said.

Krystal nodded.

She wanted to reach out and take hold of his hand, but with Heidi right there beside them, she forced herself to refrain. It had been a wonderful evening and morning, and now, she knew she had to get back to work, but she also knew she would have this on her mind all day. And she desperately wanted to call her aunt and speak with her.

"Thank you both," Krystal said when they had all finished eating, "for having me here in your lovely home, I've had a fun time."

"Can you come again?" Heidi asked with a bounce as her eyes lit up.

Krystal looked across at Anson and he smiled from Heidi and then back to Krystal.

"Well, that's up to Krystal," he grinned. "But I know I would love her to come over more often."

Krystal's heart swelled.

"I would love that," she admitted.

When they had cleared the plates away, Anson, Heidi and Krystal all loaded into the truck and headed back to the main part of town. It had been the most perfect weekend, but for now at least, there was a lot for them to think about.

Krystal sat at the counter in the store and stared into space. She had been open for around an hour, but as she had suspected, all she had managed to accomplish was daydreaming about Anson and the fact that she wanted him more than she had ever wanted anything in this world.

She tapped her cell phone and the screen shone brightly. It had been two days since she had spoken to her Aunt Beau, and although she knew she would be safe and that she had reached her friend in the German woods, she still wanted to chat with her properly and tell her of all the things that had been happening since she had been out of town.

She reached for the store phone and scrolled for Beau's mobile number in the little black book, before she punched in the digits and held the receiver up to her ear. The ring back tone was slow and strange and it took her by surprise for a moment before suddenly, there was a click and Beau's voice came down to her clear as day.

"Krystal!" her aunt said cheerily. "How the devil are you?"

Krystal laughed.

"I'm good, Aunt B," she grinned. "How are you? It's so good to hear your voice."

"And yours, my dear, and yours…" she continued, and it sounded as if she was moving into a quieter space and closing a door behind her. "How is everything going at the store? Have you managed to burn it to the ground yet?" she laughed.

"No, luckily for you, it's still standing… for now anyway."

Beau laughed and it made Krystal miss her even more.

"I need advice Auntie," she admitted. "I feel like I'm getting myself into a whole world of trouble."

The line stayed silent for a moment, and then Beau cleared her throat.

"Okay," she said in a tone that Krystal couldn't decipher. "Please, carry on…"

Krystal took a deep breath and quickly debated how to continue.

"You know how Mom always warned me away from this place?" she decided to spit it out was the only way.

"Yes," her aunt replied, again with a tone she couldn't make out whether it was warm or cold.

"Well, she always told me about the men here… the shifters… the bears… and… and…" Krystal stopped and rubbed her forehead. Even the thought of beginning to speak about it was giving her anxiety, but she couldn't hold onto these feelings alone for much longer. She needed answers and she needed to know how she could move forward.

"It's okay," Beau said. "You can tell me…"

Krystal sighed with relief and nodded to herself.

"Okay, here goes…" she said, bracing herself. "Mom

always warned me off the shifters and told me that Bridge Hollow was dangerous for me. That I shouldn't come back here and whatever I did I should never get involved with a man like that because they were dangerous. But I've been back in town for two weeks and I've met someone, Aunt Beau… He's incredible, he's everything I never knew I needed and I'm falling for him fast. He's been so respectful, and we have spoken about it all, he knows I know he's a shifter and he has told me what'll happen if we decide to move forward. I don't want to disrespect my mother's wishes… but I can't ignore these feelings. They are too strong. They are too much for me to handle. I love him already and I feel as if our souls have been connected. What am I going to do?"

Beau went quiet and Krystal could feel that her aunt was mulling things over, but she never could have predicted what came next.

"I want you to stay where you are and not to worry," Beau said calmly. "There is so much I need to tell you… and I don't want to do it over the phone."

"But… I'm here and I can't get to you," Krystal said, tears pricking the corners of her eyes.

"I'm coming to you," Beau said. "I'm coming back tonight. Okay? I want you to stay calm and not to worry, please don't drive yourself mad with guilt or feel anything other than what your heart is telling you. Do you understand me?"

Krystal was so confused, but she nodded and told her yes.

"This man, he will be for you, darling…" Aunt Beau said. "But there are a few things I should explain first."

"Okay," Krystal nodded. "Okay… I'll wait for you."

"Yes, you must…," Aunt Beau said. "Don't go running away or freaking out because you are feeling things this intensely."

The line began to crackle, and Beau cursed under her breath.

"The signal," she managed to say before the line became even fainter and Krystal could barely hear her at all. "It's breaking up. I'm in the forest... be... later... tonight..." The static was muffling her exact words, but Krystal ended the call and then flopped forward so that her head rested on the table in front of her.

Now, she was even more confused.

Would it have been easier if she had told her aunt that she had fallen for Anson, and for her to scream and shout and tell her no? For her aunt to ask her to wait for her, to tell her she was on the next flight home made her even more concerned.

What could she possibly have to explain to her that she couldn't say over the phone?

Krystal groaned into the wooden countertop and kicked her feet lightly against the legs of the high stool she was sitting on. What a total mess her life was becoming. She had moved back to Bridge Hollow hoping for answers, and all it seemed to be doing was throwing more questions her way.

She thought of Anson and of how when she had come to town, she could never have even entertained the idea of being with a shifter. But since she had met him, it had been all she could think about and all she wanted. It consumed her every waking moment, it played on her mind, even when she was sleeping. It crept into her dreams and nagged at her like a toothache, and she couldn't just forget it.

She thought of the night before, of how perfect it had been, and of the morning they had shared as a three, just her, Anson and Heidi. Now, she knew what she wanted, and she could tell that her aunt wasn't against what she was wanting to do, but was there something serious she needed to know before she went ahead and gave up her heart to Anson?

She had to wait and make sure.

She lifted her head and huffed with a pout before she dragged herself up and off the stool and toward one of the displays. There was plenty she could be doing to distract herself, but she had a long time to go before her aunt would arrive back in town. And she knew she wasn't prepared to go that long without seeing Anson again.

She reached for her cell phone out of her back pocket and scrolled to find his number. When his name illuminated the screen, she felt warm and fuzzy inside. She opened a blank message and began to type.

K: THANKS SO MUCH AGAIN FOR YESTERDAY, YOU TWO MAKE excellent hosts 😊 *If you're free later (Heidi included) I could do with some help with the basement here... And you did offer* 😊 *K x*

SHE HIT SEND AND THEN BIT HER LIP NERVOUSLY. WAS THAT being too forward? She had the feeling it wouldn't matter even if it was. Anson had made his feelings perfectly clear, and it was surely only a matter of time before they were going to have to talk about it again.

Since he had left her side, she had felt like a part of her was missing. She physically craved him. While she had been at the house with him and Heidi, she had felt so completely at peace. And now she was alone again, in the shop and working, it was as if all she could do was think about being with him again. She wanted to be swept up in his arms, she wanted to lay her head against his chest. She wanted to feel whole again, and she had done when she had been with him.

Her phone beeped and she looked at it to see that she had a reply. A little grin flitted across her lips.

· · ·

A: At your service, Madam... I'll be there for 6pm. Heidi is with my aunt later, so you'll just have to settle for me... Hope that's not a problem 😔

Krystal grinned and found herself punching the air with excitement. She was going to see him again, and for the first time since the day they had met, they were going to be properly alone.

The idea made her skin tingle with need and her heart race. She was going to have to make sure she brought her best willpower to the table and didn't get caught up in the moment, even though she knew that was going to be pretty much impossible.

Her aunt's words rumbled through her mind...

This man, he will be for you, darling...But there are a few things I should explain first...

"He will be for you..." she whispered to herself.

She slipped her phone back into her pocket and wrapped her arms around herself. She had never felt so sure of someone... Anson had been waiting for her... And she had been looking for him her whole life. Now that they had found each other, there was going to be no stopping them. She could tell her aunt knew it too... But there was still something from her past that had been hidden, she could feel it.

She couldn't be apart from him until Aunt Beau returned, but she would have to do her best to respect her wishes.

It was going to be a tough twenty-four hours. But as they say... The best things in life are worth waiting for.

CHAPTER 12

When the clock struck six, Krystal was already pacing the floor of the store, wringing her hands together and wondering how on Earth she was going to stick to her word.

She had always been so good at doing what she was told. But now that she had met Anson, she had the feeling he was going to be the exception to every rule.

She watched the door intently and had left the candles burning and the fairy lights glowing overhead, they made the place shine softly and made it all feel very romantic, and she was already feeling the love in the room before he had arrived.

When she saw his truck pull up out the front and him step out of the driver's side, her whole body felt warm and tender. Since she had left him that morning it was like she had forgotten what he looked like, she had tried to conjure him in her mind, but the details of his face would slip away. Seeing him again, at the way his deep brown eyes glinted amber when they rested on hers, the way his hair was shaggy and coarse, and the way his muscles flexed when he moved, it was all too much for her to handle.

"Hey," he said smoothly as he walked through the door and came straight toward her.

The tug between them began and it made her gasp. Feeling him being drawn to her like this was such an intense feeling, it was an experience she never could have predicted.

"Hey," she smiled, breathlessly.

She could see the look in his eyes, the want and the lust. The animal was inside him and it wanted to break free, but Anson was doing his best to subdue it.

"I missed you," she said, and his eyes glistened a little more.

"I missed you too," he smiled. "I've done nothing but think about you all day."

"Same here," she admitted. "It's been driving me crazy."

Anson reached Out and let his fingertips brush against hers.

"I spoke to my aunt," she whispered, as if she were afraid someone else was in the room and they were listening. "She's on her way home tonight."

Anson smiled. "I'm glad she's coming back," he said. "Has her trip gone well?"

"I don't really know," Krystal half laughed. "I've been so wrapped up in me and you I haven't really asked her."

"Terrible niece," he winked.

"I am, aren't I?" she laughed.

He slipped his fingers up in hers.

"Heidi is totally in awe of you," he said. "I've never seen her like this with anyone before. She's talking about you nonstop, asking when we are seeing Krystal again. My aunt is practically doing cartwheels over the moon she's so excited."

He laughed and shook his head.

"I think mine is going to be too," Krystal grinned. "But she said she needs to talk to me first."

Anson turned his eyes toward the ceiling and nodded.

"Sounds about right," he said with a half laugh. "Everyone has a take on us... I didn't figure Beau to be one of them though..."

"I don't think she is," Krystal said. "I think she's trying to reassure me... I was brought up a certain way, but I have the feeling she had something to tell me, something that will change everything I have been led to believe up until this point."

Anson raised his eyebrows and pulled her toward him.

Their bodies rubbed up against each other's, and Krystal ached for him from her head to her toes. She rested her hands on the loops of his jeans, tucking her fingers into his belt and biting her bottom lip, trying not to look at his mouth, the sexy stubble on his jaw, and the way he was so clearly hot for her it was driving him as mad as it was driving her.

"This is hard," he breathed out. "So. Fucking. Hard."

"It is for me too," she said, her mouth opening slightly, wanting so badly to kiss him.

His hand reached up and cupped her cheek and he pressed his chin into her forehead and held her close. Being there in his arms felt so safe. The protection that came from him was soothing, and she easily could have stayed there forever.

When she looked up to him and his eyes were fixed on her, she knew she didn't want to wait any longer. She simply couldn't. Whatever her aunt had to tell her, was going to have to just wait... and she would deal with the conse-quences later.

"Kiss me," she whispered.

Anson's fingers stroked her neck and she trembled. The

sensation of his rough hands at her throat was sending her into a mess of desire. Her pussy ached and she was already soaking wet for him, longing for him to rip off her clothes and take her right there and then over the desk in the middle of the store.

"Are you sure?" he whispered. "If I do, I'll imprint on you."

"I'm sure," she said as she pushed herself up on her tiptoes.

Their lips met and when he parted hers with his tongue and slipped it into her mouth, he took her breath away. The energy around them seemed to explode with passion and possibility, and she felt something forge between them. Something strong and binding, something that had been brewing since the moment they had both been born.

His big arms gripped hold of her and she could feel his strength. He was such a big, muscular man, and she felt tiny next to him, but he was making her feel so safe and secure, none of that mattered.

She wrapped her arms up and around his neck, kissing him deeply and melting into him, never wanting the moment to end.

When their lips finally broke apart and she looked into his eyes, they were completely golden, and his pupils were dark and wide. He was panting and she could see the change in him, the animal was coming to the surface, but it didn't frighten her.

He wrapped his arms around her shoulders and pulled her in close. They were both breathless and wanting more... but they knew they had to wait.

The kiss was just the beginning... he had imprinted on her now and she was marked as his. But to claim her, that was going to be the ultimate commitment, one that would join them together as soul mates until the end of time.

Being so close to him and not being able to have him, was

a new pain all its own. Krystal had to exercise the most willpower she had ever had in her life. To distract themselves, they started to work at the task at hand… the store. They wandered to the doorway of the basement and she opened the door to show Anson inside. The icy blast of air came hurtling toward them and he squinted his eyes as if to shield them from it.

"There are barely any lights down there…" she said. "Could you help me find some extras?"

Anson was staring intently ahead, but he didn't seem to have heard her.

"The cold," he said as he shivered. "I've never known it to be like this."

Krystal grasped around for the light cord and pulled it. The small bulb above them came buzzing to life and the sinister staircase came into view ahead of them. It really was a terrifying sight, especially at night, and she was glad to have someone else there with her or she never would dare go down there.

Anson smiled at her weakly, as if he had a bad feeling, but then he turned on the light on his cell phone and shone it further into the opening of the earth below.

"I've owned this building for years," he said. "And I've never known it to feel like this."

"With the cold?"

He nodded.

"I've only felt cold like this once before around here…" he seemed instantly wary. "And trust me… it wasn't good."

"I came down here the other day and it was exactly the same… it was so chilling I almost couldn't stand it. My legs ached after I had come back up to the store." Krystal told him.

Anson sniffed the air and she saw the amber return to his eyes. She was sure she heard a low growl come from deep inside him and it took her aback. She stepped away and watched how he became more animalistic, his shoulders hunched up and he growled again.

"Anson?" she said with worry. "Are you okay?"

"Step back," he said, but his voice had changed, it was deeper and gruffer, and it was muddled in amongst a roar.

She gasped and moved quickly out of the way, back through the doorway and into the hall, looking into the basement entrance a the large stone steps that ran deep below.

Anson growled again and he turned and looked at her, his eyes flashed menacingly, but she wasn't afraid. There was something about this that made her feel calm, as if she knew he was in control and if he had to shift, then it would be for a good reason.

She watched as he rose up high from a crouching position, and then she gasped and clung to the wall behind her and watched in a vague sort of enchanted horror as his clothing and skin began to rip apart and fur sprang up in its place. The bear was growling, and Anson's human shape was quickly morphing. To watch it happen in front of her very eyes was exhilarating, but she also knew she had to keep her distance, she wasn't yet sure what he was capable of… would she be in danger from him when he was like this? Or would he still be able to keep control of himself and not let the animal completely take over?

Anson screamed and let out a guttural roar as the dark, brown fur whipped around his entire body, he grew to almost twice his size and was so massive and hulking that he blocked out the light coming from the doorway.

Krystal's heart was pounding, and she was breathing so quickly she couldn't hear anything over the thumping of her heart and her own ragged breath. She reached out and let her fingertips skim his fur and she smiled, she felt a connection to him still and she knew then she was safe.

"He imprinted," she whispered to herself.

He had marked her as his, whether he had fully claimed her yet or not... he was bound to her now, and he was committed to her protection. She smiled and held her hand on her heart.

Anson growled and rose to his hind legs. He was now fully the bear and his jaws were wide and massive as he roared into the basement. The chill from deep within kept getting stronger and stronger, so much so that she felt as if her fingers were beginning to freeze.

She watched as Anson's sniffed the air again and then he charged down the stone steps, breaking off pieces of wall from either side as he went. The building seemed to shake, and Krystal screamed but held her own out there. She clung to the wall by her fingertips and closed her eyes, just hoping and praying that something more terrible than her grizzly shifter boyfriend wasn't about to come crawling back out of the basement and rip her into pieces.

Below, she could hear banging and crashing, the bear was roaring, but apart from him there wasn't another sound.

Suddenly, it all went quiet, and Krystal waited for a moment, wiping the tears from her eyes and composing herself before she stepped forward on shaking legs.

She peered in the doorway and at the crumbled walls and broken stone steps. As a bear, he must weigh so much that he had completely broken them and the stone was scattered all around the base of the staircase.

"Anson?" she whispered.

Her voice seemed to echo down there, and she tried to pick up the courage to move to the top step, but she didn't know if it would collapse if she did.

"Anson?" she asked again.

The silence seemed to be deafening. It consumed her and

her heart was racing so powerfully it was causing her ears to ring and her head to spin.

Finally, there was a noise from below, as if someone was moving wood and earth, and then a massive heave as if something had been pushed over. She moved back against the wall and closed her eyes.

Should she run? Or should she stay?

Her intuition was telling her that Anson was all right, she could still feel him, and she didn't want to run. If she were to be with him, then this would be her life. She had gotten used to the concept of shifters long ago… but actually seeing one turn in front of her was another ball game entirely, and she knew it was going to take her some time to adapt.

She breathed out and tried to focus.

"Anson?" she said again.

"I'm okay…" his voice broke the silence from below and she gasped and slunk against the wall, her feet giving out from beneath her with complete relief.

He coughed and she heard him moving closer, as if he were beginning to climb back up the stairs.

"Do you need help?" she asked.

"No," he replied. "I'm coming."

She clutched her arms to her chest and tried not to look too stunned and afraid, but as soon as he emerged and she saw the man she had fallen for, all her fears melted away. He was still there; he was still Anson.

He had pulled back on his ripped jeans, but his torso was completely bare, and she could see his muscles and how big and defined they were. His shoulders were broad, and they looked strong and powerful. She gulped and tried not to drool.

God was he sexy.

When he fully climbed back out and was standing in front of her, she could see instantly that he was cradling

97

something in his arms. Her heart began to pound even harder and her eyes were fixed fully on it, so much so she felt as if she could have burned holes into the top of it.

It was a book.

A big, very old looking book…

"What… what is that?" she whispered.

Anson gripped it in his hands and looked down at her before he shook his head and sighed.

"I don't think we even want to know…" he replied.

*A*nson closed the door to the basement and locked it quickly with the key before he turned and looked around for something to block the doorway. Over at the very back of the store he could see an old dresser and he moved quickly and grabbed it with his big rough hands, passing the old book to Krystal and heaving the chest with all his might.

"What are you doing?" she asked him. "What's going on?"

He looked up at her and could see the fear in her eyes. He didn't want to alarm her, and he surely didn't want to scare her away, but this was vital. He had to block the exit to the basement as best he could, and fast.

He pulled the dresser right in front of it and then he moved and started to collect the unopened boxes that were still stacked high in the back hallway. He moved as fast as he could, grabbing a box and slamming it on top of the dresser, creating a barricade so that the door wouldn't be able to be opened from the inside out.

"Anson?" Krystal said again, with a little whimper in her voice. "You're scaring me."

He leaned back against the wall and his breathing was fast

and sharp. He had used so much energy when he had shifted, he now felt weak and he was so worried he didn't know how to make it all better again.

"Okay," he said as he looked at the barricade he had made with the dresser and full boxes. "That should do. Let's go."

He grabbed hold of her hand and raced with her toward the door of the store.

"Wait!" she called. "Please let me know what's going on."

The candles and lights were still lit, but Anson's eyes kept darting back to the basement. He swallowed and rubbed his big, rough hands over his face and stubble, and he could feel the sweat pooling on his abs.

"The cold," he said, a chill running over him as he remembered it. "It's what has been happening here in Bridge Hollow just before evil stirred up… something is below us… Something bad."

Krystal's eyes widened and she moved quickly around the room blowing out the candles and grabbing her things.

"What shall we do?" she asked as she looked at the book in her hands. It felt soft, but it was icy cold. The leather was almost frozen, and it was chilling her hands to the bone.

"We need to leave," he said. "Grab what you can, we have to get out of here now."

ANSON DROVE THE TRUCK AS FAST AS HE COULD AWAY FROM the store and stopped on the other side of town. He rubbed a sweaty hand down his face and turned to look at Krystal. She looked so beautiful, but he could tell she was scared. Her breathing was rapid, and her eyes were wide like a stunned animal.

He reached over and gripped her hand to reassure her.

"We're going to be okay," he said. "But I have to get this book to my pack."

"What's inside?" she asked. She was looking at it as if she were afraid to open it.

Anson shifted in his seat and took a deep breath.

"For a while, we have had our suspicions of what has been happening here..." he began. "Connections to the old mine that collapsed over a hundred years ago... but we have never been able to find it."

She looked up at him and her eyes were so innocent, he just wanted to pull her to him and never let her go.

"My aunt is away searching for some kind of parapsychologist," she said. "She thinks that it's the spirits of the people from the mine that have come back for revenge. She thinks their spirits are still here in town... hunting us all down."

Anson shook his head.

"We thought that too at one point," he admitted. "But now... after finding this... I know the truth."

He looked at the book and reached for it.

When he had opened the door to the basement and felt the cold, he had known something was down there. His family had owned that building for decades, if not longer, and he spent a lot of time there. It was no coincidence that Beau had been drawn to it for her venture... it was clearly a hotspot for paranormal activity.

As soon as he had stepped inside and he had sniffed the air, he had known that danger was down there. He smelled all the things that had clung to the sites of the other events and tragedies that had happened over the past year. He smelled death and decay, he smelled the blood of the vampire that he and his pack had killed along with the wolves. He smelled a world that was not of his own.

His instinct had kicked in and he had raced at the spot in the basement that had been the strongest and he had turned it over, attacked it, not knowing if something was there waiting for him or whether he would destroy a wall and let something free.

And that's when he found the book.

Buried in an old safe, hidden behind the back wall of the basement.

The wall had come down so easily, he didn't know how he had never done it before. But he had never shifted into his bear form inside the building, and he had never felt what he was feeling down there like he had that day.

"This book," he said. "It has all the answers."

He opened it and squinted at the old writing in calligraphic ink. Someone had spent a lot of time creating this tomb, and it was all written there and clear for him to see.

The legend of Bridge Hollow... documented forever and written for someone to find it when the time was right.

It turned out the time was now... and that someone was him.

His eyes scanned the words and a knot formed in his throat as he read... it was so much worse than any of them had realized... and now, it was going to fall on him to break the news to the rest of the shifters of the town...

He had been chosen.

...THE SMYTH FAMILY OF EARLY BRIDGE HOLLOW MADE A PACT with the native American Indians of the area that once they purchased the land and took over that they would not dig for gold nor build on the proposed site. Many mistakes were made over those months, but ultimately, once the mining accident happened on that sacred land, a great new threat was unleashed on our world.

A veil was pierced, between good and bad... The mine opened a vortex, a place in time and space, that allowed creatures from other dimensions to travel here to us and to come into our world.

To save the planet Earth, the mine was sealed and built over, it's real location never revealed to the many people who questioned its existence over the years. The new and existing town of Bridge Hollow was fully built upon it, with this place where this book will reside, the actual gateway to the mine and therefor the other world itself.

Another mine has been created to lure wandering eyes and keep our secrets safe. Many people died that day and their families need somewhere to grieve. But it is too dangerous here. The mine they believe collapsed is located on the mountain and shall henceforth be the only mine known to have existed here on this land.

The real gateway to the other world must forever remain sealed or there will be grave consequences. It is the shifter families of Bridge Hollow, the packs of animal men, who must protect this place, and therefore the rest of the world as we know it.

Krystal was reading with him and he could feel her shaking.

"Holy shit," she whispered. "Is this all true?"

Anson looked at her and nodded, "I'm afraid so...," he said. "And now, I need to get this book to my pack, and fast. We have been looking for the mine for months and had believed it to be up on the mountain... why we weren't told of this sooner is a mystery all its own... but we have to act fast. We need to secure that gateway as best we can."

Krystal nodded and he smiled at her before he cupped her face and pulled her lips to his. He kissed her and she tasted so sweet and inviting, he had completely fallen for her and would do anything to protect her and Heidi. He had to get the book to the pack, then he had to go home and make sure that Krystal and his family were safe. He was weighted under responsibilities, but thankfully he had been there at just the right time. The cold in the basement had been so intense, it could only be a matter of hours before the next wave of evil burst through and raged hell on the town.

"Come on," he said as his eyes glinted at her. "Let's go."

She gripped his hand and it felt so good to have her by his side. He felt stronger than ever, and he knew it was down to her.

CHAPTER 14

*K*rystal's head was a complete mess as she looked across at Heidi sleeping soundly in her bed. Her cell phone was clutched in her palm and she was still shaking from all the revelations the day had brought with it. When she had called Anson and asked for help, she had no clue of what they were about to find. Sure, she knew things were happening in the town, that bad stuff had started to creep its way in and that people were scared… but never in a million years did she think she would be caught up in it to this level. That she would be right there when an ancient manuscript was discovered to explain to the shifter packs of Bridge Hollow the true extent of the threat.

Anson had brought her back to his home and had made sure that she, Heidi and his old Aunt Nora were safe. It had been an honor to meet her, and Krystal could tell that Nora was just as enamored with her as Heidi had been.

"You're his chosen one," she had said as she cupped Krystal's face and smiled at her warmly. "It's so good you have finally arrived."

Krystal felt so special, so incredibly grateful to have

105

followed her fate back to her original hometown, and now, she just hoped that it would all survive long enough for her to live and enjoy it.

Heidi rolled over and breathed deeply. She had slept the entire evening and was completely unaware that anything was happening. Krystal smiled; the innocence of a child was the most wonderful thing in the world.

She tucked her in and then stepped quietly out of the bedroom, doing her best not to wake her.

She walked slowly down the hall to the living area and sat up at the kitchen island with her phone in her hands. She had been trying to contact Beau but knew she was traveling back and was likely in the air. Every time she had dialed her number it had gone straight to voicemail as if it were turned off, and her texts had gone unanswered.

She opened another message and sent one more…

K: I KNOW YOU'RE PROBABLY ON A FLIGHT CROSSING THE ATLANTIC right now, but I just wanted to tell you again PLEASE DO NOT GO TO THE STORE OR THE APARTMENT. Something extremely dangerous is there! Come to Anson's home instead, I am here, and we are all safe. Love you xx

SHE SIGHED AS SHE PRESSED SEND AND THEN RESTED THE phone on the counter. Aunt Nora was fast asleep in one of the spare rooms downstairs, and Heidi was tucked in safely too. Now, all Krystal could do was pace until she got word from Anson. It felt as if he had been gone for hours, and he probably had. Her eyes were starting to feel weary and she looked up to the clock on the wall to see that it was just past midnight.

She rested her head in her hands and yawned.

Her energy was completely depleted, and her mind was working on overdrive. It had been such a crazy day, with so much to take in, she didn't actually know how she was still functioning.

Suddenly, a prickle worked its way up the back of her neck, and she felt the now familiar tug of longing deep within her heart. She turned and looked toward the doorway, and she could feel him out there somewhere close to the house.

Anson was making his way home.

She smiled and got to her feet and gripped the side of the island, hoping to god that he was all right. Her lips burned and tingled with the fire and energy of their kiss, he was still lingering on her skin, and his power was still coursing through her.

The door started to unlock from the inside and the handle turned, and when it opened, and they lay eyes on each other they both ran down the hallway until their bodies collided and they were holding each other in a deep and desperate embrace.

"Are you okay?" he asked, his breath hot and heavy.

"I'm fine," she whispered. "Are you? What happened?"

She pulled back and looked at him all over. He didn't seem to be hurt in any way, his eyes still glinted with amber, but he was settled and in some way at peace.

"I took the book to my pack," he said. "And we did the best we could."

He took her hand and led her back into the back half of the house, his broad shoulders were slightly slumped, and he looked exhausted. Krystal made her way to the refrigerator and pulled out a bottle of water and some food. She set down a big plate of sliced meat, one that he had cooked a day before, and she urged him to eat.

"You look worn out," she said as she grabbed him a plate. "Here."

Anson unscrewed the top of the bottle and drank the whole thing quickly and in what appeared to only be three large gulps. He set it down and wiped his mouth and then he pulled the plate toward him and started to eat the meat. He was ravenous, she could see it, and it was clear the animal inside him was desperate to be nourished.

When he had finished, he pulled her onto his knee and kissed her neck. He wrapped his arms around her from behind and held her there as if he never wanted to let her go.

"What happened?" she whispered.

"We went to the store," he said. "And we did what we could."

"Is the veil sealed?" she asked.

Anson shook his head.

"We read over the tomb and sent for another pack that lives at the top of the mountains. They have been an ancient and much needed force here since the accident happened, but they have had to stay out of plain sight and well away from any humans. They are dragons… Men who shift into a beast that has never been believed. It would be absolute carnage is a tourist or a resident of our town saw one of these men when he was shifted into his true form. It is easy to explain away a large wolf or a bear… But a Dragon?" he laughed and shook his head. "It would blow people's minds."

Krystal nodded. She felt like she was having her mind blown right now. She had never heard of a Dragon shifter before… And the idea was more than terrifying.

"We met them there at the store with the wolf pack, and we discussed our next steps. We all agreed that the entire building has to be sealed and guarded from now on, until we figure out a way to defeat this thing."

"So… my aunt…?" she asked.

"Everything inside had potentially been touched by evil," he told her sadly. "We need to barricade it all in and wait."

"So, my aunt will have to close the store?" she asked.

Anson nodded.

"For now, the precautions we have taken with the basement will hold… But it's what could happen later, when the forces get stronger or they figure out a way around what we have already done. Things have been slipping through all year, and we still believe that there must be an area in up the mountain and in the forest where the veil is also thin, maybe an old tunnel of the mine that had been long forgotten but is still hidden beneath the earth."

He kissed her neck and again and it sent shivers up her spine. She had never been kissed like that by a man, and it felt so erotic. Her pussy ached and she turned her head to look at him over her shoulder, a little smile flitting across her lips.

"I was so worried," she whispered. "I just wanted you back here with us."

He smiled and nudged his forehead against hers.

"Heidi has slept soundly, and your aunt too… I have been checking on them."

"Thank you," he said. "I honestly don't know how I have survived without you for this long."

They both laughed.

"I could say exactly the same," Krystal whispered.

She slipped from his knee and turned to face him. He pulled her between his legs and wrapped his big, protective arms around her. She looked into his eyes and their lips met. His kiss was powerful and hungry, and it made her moan with desire.

Their lips broke apart and they stared into each other's eyes. There was nothing quite like the potential end of the world to make someone want to live in the moment. Krystal moved backward and took his hand.

"Take me upstairs," she whispered, and she knew her eyes were large and engulfed with want.

Anson rose to his feet and looked down at her. He pushed his body up against hers and she could feel the hard poke of his desire pressing into her belly.

She bit her lip and pulled him again, urging him to take her toward the staircase.

In one swift movement, he pulled her up and wrapped her legs around his waist as he stared into her eyes and walked with her to the stairs. He kissed her, nibbling her neck and sending her pleasure into overdrive with each step. She was so wet for him, and they hadn't even made it to the bedroom.

At the top of the landing, he moved down and away from Heidi's room to the other side of the house, where he kicked a door open with the tip of his boot and carried her inside. He was so strong, and he held her effortlessly as he closed the door behind him and then walked with her to the bed.

He lay her down and stood above her, looking at her. Krystal's heart was in her mouth and her body was already trembling and full of anticipation. She knew what this would mean, but it was more than perfect, and she knew now it wouldn't matter what her aunt told her... She wanted to be here, and she wanted to be with him. Nothing had felt so right before, and she wasn't prepared to walk away from it, no matter what the cost.

She opened her legs and bit her lip, waiting for him to come to her. He pulled his t-shirt off over his head and his massive, heavy muscles throbbed in front of her and she gasped. He was so manly and so strong; she knew that the moment he could have her, she was going to be completely at his mercy.

He slid his hand and between her legs to separate them further, before slipping between them and putting his full weight on her. He rubbed himself on her, pressing his crotch against hers and quickly moving to unbutton his jeans. He leaned back and pulled them down, showing his boxer shorts and the mammoth, hard bulge inside them. Krystal gulped, but her pussy throbbed again, excited to see what he was hiding. He took her knees and then moved toward her jeans. He unbuttoned them one by one, and then pulled them down and slid them off before he threw them over his shoulder. He pressed down on her again and she could feel him, big and hard inside his boxers. The feeling of him pressed against her was exquisite and she gasped as a wave of pleasure pulsed through her, making her gush in her panties.

"I want you, Krystal," he panted. "I need to be inside you."

She moaned and nodded, she wanted nothing more than to take his huge cock inside her, and when he reached for her underwear and pulled them down, she gasped and opened her legs wider. He slowly slipped an enormous finger inside her as she writhed against him and moaned with pleasure.

He pinned one of her wrists to the pillows above and with her free hand, she moved it down to his crotch, groping for him until she pulled down his underwear. When she first managed to wrap her hand around his incredible cock, she couldn't believe how big he was. She had never been with a man who was that size before and she was suddenly scared… How was she going to take him? He was so big and powerful, and her pussy was so tight… Surely, he was going to destroy her? But she was so overcome with arousal that she wouldn't turn back, she wanted him so badly and she wanted to be claimed. Anson groaned and moved between her legs so that his massive length was positioned at her pussy. He looked at her deep in the eyes and pressed himself into her, penetrating her inch by inch, opening her wider than she had ever been. She gasped, the pleasure rippling through her as he thrust himself in and out, his intense heat filling her up and making them one. She felt weightless and as if he were taking her to new levels of pleasure. He gripped her breasts and kissed her neck as he slid his cock in and out of her dripping wet pussy. His arms were heavy and hairy, his groans turned to growls, getting louder, deeper and gruffer. He was taking on another persona and his whole demeanor was changing the more pleasure he experienced. Krystal's world was a haze of thrusts and growls. She opened herself up to him like a flower, his hot, hard cock pumping in and out of her and bringing her to the edge of the most intense release. She gripped him, and her whole body tensed up as he thrust again, hitting her spot so hard and good she knew she could not hold on any longer. She fell back in an explosive rush of pleasure, just as she felt Anson's body tense and jerk, and he growled so ferociously at the ceiling that it made her cum even harder. He emptied his massive load in her pussy, gripping her as the heat rose from deep within him. Her whole body spasmed as she came, biting his shoulder and as she did another roar came from him, the power along with it so impressive, she knew that from then on, something between them had changed. She felt the bond grow, the fate spinning out ahead of them. In an instant she knew she was his, and what she had been waiting for had finally happened… Anson had claimed her.

He collapsed on top of her and held her in his arms. She looked into his eyes and she saw the animal inside them. The amber was shining from within, the bear was in there and now, she belonged to them both. She kissed him hard on the mouth and he held her throat lightly as he kissed her back and they lay together in the aftermath of their love.

This experience had changed them both forever… and now, they would never be alone again. Anson and Krystal had found each other, they had bonded together, and now, they were family.

He held her from behind all night long and kissed the back of her neck as they fell to sleep. They were both exhausted after the events of the day, and now that they had sealed their relationship and made it official, it was clear that they were going to need some serious recovery time. Making love had never been so life changing.

CHAPTER 15

The next morning, she woke to the sound of chatter coming from downstairs and she reached to Anson's side of the bed to discover that he had gone. She sat up and scowled, momentarily disappointed that he had left her there, until she saw a small handwritten note on the end of the bed...

COME DOWN WHEN YOU'RE READY. BREAKFAST WILL BE WAITING...

SHE SMILED AND HELD IT AGAINST HER CHEST. NO ONE HAD ever treated her so well. It was as if she was a princess and starring in her own personal fairy tale... Instead of the prince, she had been rescued by a mountain man bear. She laughed. Her life was certainly very different to what it had been a month before.

Gulped bShe climbed out of bed and wrapped herself in the robe that was hanging on the back of the door. She went into the adjoining backroom and ran the faucet, splashed her face with water and took a swig of mouthwash. Considering she had spent the majority of the night being thrown around the bedroom, she looked surprisingly fresh, and her skin was rosy. She saw her eyes were glinting in a way they never had before, and she felt a pang in her heart as she realized they mirrored Anson's.

"I'm his now," she whispered to herself as she moved to the bedroom and quickly dressed.

She ran her hands through her long, dark hair and shook it over her shoulders before she reached for the door handle and opened it and stepped into the hall.

As she walked to the stairs, she realized that it wasn't just Anson's and Heidi's voices that she could hear in the kitchen. She could also hear Aunt Nora… and another woman…

Her heart skipped a beat and she picked up her pace, racing toward the staircase and running down them two at a time. She slid down the hallway, rounded the corner and entered the kitchen, and when she saw who was standing there, she almost collapsed with relief.

"Aunt Beau," she panted as she dashed to her and flung her arms around her.

Her aunt looked as elegant as ever, standing tall with her long silver hair, wearing her purple shawl and all her crystals and rings.

"Oh, Krystal," she whispered. "I am so glad to be back."

"I'm so glad you're here," Krystal sobbed into her shoulder. "It has been a wild ride here while you've been gone."

"So I hear," her aunt mused.

Anson was leaning against the counter, and he smiled and tried not to laugh.

Krystal looked at him over Beau's shoulder and he winked, and then he moved forward and reached for her hand and pulled her close to him. He kissed her on the lips and smiled, looking at her deep in the eyes.

"Good morning," he said so only the two of them could hear.

She smiled at him and felt so completely at peace, it was as if she had finally found the place she was supposed to be. Right here, on this morning, with him...

Heidi was bouncing around the kitchen and living area, completely ecstatic to have a house full of women and laughter, and she and old Aunt Nora seemed genuinely happy about the new developments happening with Anson and Krystal.

"Come on, now, Heidi," Aunt Nora said. "Let's get you dressed and ready for school."

Anson silently thanked her, and the two of them moved out of the room and toward the stairs.

Krystal smiled as she watched them go, and then she turned to face Anson and Krystal and smiled at them both as well.

"Well, I see you couldn't wait for me to get home," she teased.

Krystal felt her face flush pink and she bit her lip to hide her grin.

"But I'm just glad you didn't run in the other direction, that was what I was afraid of."

Krystal cocked her head to the side, unsure of what was coming next.

"The only reason I asked you to wait for me, is because there is something you need to know."

Krystal felt her stomach drop and she tensed up. She had been dreading hearing this... was her entire world about to come crashing down?

Anson wrapped his arm around her shoulder protectively, as if he were expecting the same thing. And Krystal looked up at him nervously.

"Krystal," her aunt continued. "Your mother did take you

away from Bridge Hollow when you were a child to keep you away from the magic and the men that were here…" she trailed off and Anson scowled. He clearly wasn't enjoying what he was hearing.

"But she told you this was because of the fact that the shifter men were trouble," her aunt went on. "But… this isn't exactly true."

Krystal's eyes were wide and expectant, waiting for Aunt Beau to lower the boom.

"Your mother and I, we always did have a connection to the paranormal side of life, and we have always been able to see and know things. When she was not much younger than you, she fell very much in love with a man of Bridge Hollow… a shifter wolf."

Krystal's eyes were wide, and she couldn't believe what she was hearing. She had always thought that her mother was so against shifters because her own parents had warned her off them… because she had seen them do terrible things and that they had hurt her in some way. But if this was the case, then why had she fallen in love with one?

"What happened?" she asked.

"Your mother was young… She loved him with all her heart, but even then, this place was on shaky ground and terrible things can happen between packs." Aunt Beau stopped and swallowed; her eyes flitted to Anson before she got the courage to continue.

"You mother's shifter wolf love was killed in an inter-pack war," she said with a sigh. "He was brutally murdered, and it drew a line between the two packs there and then. It was always thought that it would never be overcome, that the shifters would be at odds with each other for the rest of time. But as I grew older, as my powers developed, I began to see another side of the magic of this town."

Krystal's heart was thumping.

"Your mother moved on as best she could… She started dating again, and she met your father and they had you. But her heart always belonged to her shifter wolf. She had been claimed by him and was so unhappy without him. She couldn't bear it."

Krystal's eyes filled with tears. Knowing what she now did about the power of the love between her and Anson, she could only imagine how distressing it must have been for her mother to lose hers.

How had she never told her about this?

"When your father absconded and left you both, she couldn't bear to be here anymore. The memories were all too painful, everywhere she turned, she saw the bear and dragon packs that had killed the love of her life, the other part of her soul. And then, I had my vision…"

"Your vision?" Krystal asked.

Anson was still holding her, and she felt safe with him. She knew he wasn't the reason now for her aunt being wary, and she was so relieved to hear that her mother had once loved a shifter too.

"Yes," Aunt Beau said. "I saw the future of this place… And it had you in it."

Krystal watched her eagerly, waiting for her to continue.

"You and a shifter bear were to be part of the salvation of Bridge Hollow. My vision told me that you were the fated mate of one of the bears that resided here… and your mother was so distressed by this that she packed your things and you both left for the city. She had had her heart broken by the war and rivalries in this town, and she loved you so much she couldn't bear for you to go through the same. She didn't want you to get hurt, she didn't want the love of your life to be taken from you… but as time passed by and I told her of all the changes here, how the bears and the wolves had mended old ways and were existing side by side without violence, it was then she told me that when the time was right, it would be your turn to return here to Bridge Hollow."

Krystal's skin was tingling, and a shiver ran up her spine. She had been called home, and her mother hadn't disapproved.

"Why did she never tell me herself?" Krystal asked.

"Because she was taken from us too soon," her Aunt Beau said sadly. "Your mother was a fantastic, amazing woman... and it was a loss for the world when her light was extinguished so young."

Krystal felt a tear roll down her cheek. She missed her mom so much and to hear all of this was breaking her heart. To know her mom had loved a shifter and had been claimed, only to have him taken from her was devastating... but now Krystal was back to carry on their family legacy. And she was determined to make her mother proud.

"Thank you," she said as she wiped away the tear. "Thank you for telling me."

Anson kissed the side of her head and looked down at her with adoring eyes. The emotions in the room were high and she felt beaten and bruised, but she still wouldn't want to be anywhere else.

She finally knew the truth.

Her mother had been trying to protect her from a broken heart. But in doing so, she had eventually paved the way for Krystal to follow her fate, and it had all worked out exactly how it was supposed to.

Her and Anson had both met broken, but now, they had joined together and were finally healed.

Aunt Beau smiled at them and bowed a little, holding her hands together at her chest.

"I'll leave you two to talk," she whispered. "But I am so happy to see you both together. You really are meant to be..."

She turned and walked toward the doorway and Krystal looked up at Anson. At her man… her shifter bear.

It certainly had been a wild ride since she had arrived in Bridge Hollow. But she had found her rightful place in the world… and now, she had found the love of her life too…

She truly was one of the lucky ones.

Now, she had it all.

CHAPTER 16

Bridge Hollow, Two Weeks Later

KRYSTAL STOOD AT THE SIDE OF THE ROAD, LOOKING OUT across Main Street and at the paranormal store. It was still hard to see it this way, but she knew there was no other way it could be right now. The bears, wolves and dragons had all secured it. To the unknowing eye, it just looked as if it had been boarded over and a sign read CLOSED FOR RENOVA-TION on the front door. But inside was another story... Inside, it was a battle ground waiting to happen.

Sheets of enforced steel had been placed in the basement to line the walls and floors. The door had been nailed shut and more steel had been placed over it. The barricades were still in place and the whole building was on lockdown, complete with all of Krystal's and Beau's belongings inside.

She sighed and scratched the side of her neck. It was upsetting to know that the place her aunt had set up shop was also the site of an ancient threat. Sacred land that had been tampered with and cursed forever when the mine had collapsed, and the veil had been opened.

But she was glad it had happened to them and not to anyone else. Another resident of Bridge Hollow likely wouldn't have been strong enough to handle the responsibility. And Krystal had been part of the prophecy after all... Her aunt had seen in a vision many years before that Krystal and her shifter bear soul mate would be part of the town's salvation... and it had been them that had discovered the ancient manuscript and the gateway to the other world.

Main Street was bustling and full of activity. The rest of Bridge Hollow had no idea what had happened around them only a couple of weeks before, and they were all busy celebrating Halloween. The whole town had been decorated, pumpkins lined every street, witches and ghosts hung from the trees, and fake blood dripped from the windows of the shops along with fake signs saying ZOMBIE NEST – DO NOT ENTER.

It was a good feeling to know that life was still continuing. They may have been under threat, but the town was still alive... and no one was going to take away their happiness just yet.

Krystal saw Anson and Heidi down the street walking toward her. Heidi was dressed as a witch and had insisted on a long black wig so she could look as much like Krystal as possible. She had even wanted a nose ring, but both Anson and Krystal had both decided even a fake one would be crossing the line at age five.

Krystal smiled at the memory. It felt good to have a family of her own... and they were all bonded so fast and real, she finally felt as if she had lay her demons to rest.

Anson and Heidi approached her, and he wrapped his arm around her shoulder. Heidi bounced up and down with her trick or treating bag and shook it so Krystal could see all the candy she had managed to collect on her hunt up and down Main Street.

"Are you ready?" Anson smiled as he looked at Krystal.

She smiled and nodded.

"Let's go…," she said.

They walked hand in and further down the street and crossed back over once they had gotten well past the paranormal store. The shifters had told everyone to give it a wide berth, and the rumors running around town were that they had an insect infestation and needed specialist treatment to the old wood inside. The people of the town were so proud of their little part of the world that they wouldn't do anything to jeopardize it, and they had all agreed that the store should be boarded and left alone until the problem was resolved.

Shifters Bliss had its main door thrown open and from inside Krystal heard the thumping of music, but this time, it was of a different kind. Disney and kids' songs rang out onto the street and the exterior had been decorated with tons of Halloween decorations… Making the place look like a haunted house.

"Has Ryder actually gone mad?" Anson laughed. "This is so unlike him… throwing a kid's party in our bar…"

"Maybe he has seen what we all have these past few weeks," Krystal said warmly. "That the future is important, and we need to look after it."

Anson squeezed her hand and smiled.

Heidi bounced through the door and ran off into the crowd to find her friends. She started dancing with a group of boys and girls from her class at school, and Anson and Krystal stood in the doorway watching them.

There were many familiar faces in the bar. The wolves, the bears… Even a dragon had made an appearance… The town was fully united to celebrate this one night before the annual festival rolled to town and they were thrown into a new sea of activity.

Krystal looked at Anson and his eyes glinted amber, and she knew hers would be doing the same.

Two hearts had become one. Two souls had connected. And one major legacy was being fulfilled.

Bridge Hollow was as lucky as they were.

For now, at least, the town was safe.

* * *

We hope you loved this tale! If so please check out the next story in the Bridge Hollow series...

CLICK HERE TO GET CLAIMED BY THE ALPHA DRAGON HERE ON Amazon

FINE...WE HAVE A PREVIEW FOR YOU ;) ...

WINTER HAD DESCENDED UPON THE TOWN, BRINGING WITH IT A new darkness; the likes of which Braxton and his father, Bishop, had never seen. For months, their town had been under threat, and now, at what was going to be the busiest time of year, they were being thrown into a whole new wave of uncertainty.

Braxton stood on the balcony outside his bedroom and looked out over the forest surrounding him and his family. They had lived high in the mountains of Bridge Hollow for decades, guarding the areas they believed to be in danger. The cursed land in the area had been hidden away, and they believed they were the ones who were protecting it. But as recent events had unfolded, they had found out that all was not as it seemed…

Braxton crossed his arms over his chest and flexed his muscles. He had a power inside of him, strong and severe; one that was always threatening to escape, but one he was also used to controlling. A fire raged beneath his skin, and of all the shifters that had lived in Bridge Hollow, he and his family were some of the strongest.

They were dragons. Powerful creatures that were believed to be fantasy. They stayed high in those mountains and out of sight so that no wandering tourists would spot them on those moments when their guards were slightly down, or their inner beasts were being too playful, and they had to shift. Shifting into the animal inside of him gave Braxton an energy and passion that was indescribable. But he was still wary of when and where he could use it. Their town and all the magic within it had lived so peacefully because they were good at hiding their powers. If humans were to catch them, it would be disastrous. Large bears and wolves roaming the mountains and the land below could easily be explained.

But a dragon was another story. They had to be kept out of sight and hidden away, however isolating it may be.

Braxton clenched his jaw. He felt tense and nervous, as if he could sense a storm on its way. He sniffed the air and looked to the night's sky and at all the stars overhead. It was a dark night, and there was no moon in sight, which always made him uneasy. He looked to the moon for guidance on many occasions, and when it wasn't present, he felt an impending sense of doom.

"Brax?" his father's voice cut in from behind him, and Braxton turned to face him.

Even though his father, Bishop, was almost one-hundred

years old, he wasn't an old man in any sense of the word. In fact, he looked more like he was in his fifties by human standards, with salt and pepper hair and a dashingly perfect smile. Braxton looked up to him with awe, and knew that if his father's genes were anything to go by, he too would age exceptionally well and continue to live life to the fullest, even when he had been on the planet for almost a century.

"Hi, Dad," Braxton smiled.

Bishop sidled up next to him and sighed. They had both had a week filled with sleepless nights, but now, the final evening before the town sprang into action had finally arrived. Braxton would have been exhausted had it not been for his dragon blood, but with the fire running through him, he was nothing but alert and sharp as a knife.

"Dawn isn't far away," Bishop said. "The bears and wolves have been in touch, and they want us to check the mountains one last time."

Braxton nodded.

He was always ready to go out and hunt. To try and track down any danger that may be lurking in the shadows, threatening their world.

"And the tourists?" Braxton asked. "Have they started to arrive?"

His father shook his head.

"A few, here and there, but not too many, so far."

Braxton felt a little swell of relief fill him. But it still wasn't going to change the outcome… Come tomorrow, the town would be full of strangers. Innocent people looking for a good time, completely unaware that they were walking into the middle of a multidimensional war.

Bishop patted his son on the shoulder and turned to walk back into their mountaintop mansion. Braxton watched him leave and gave a weak smile as the door closed behind him and he was once again alone with the night. He looked back to the stars and breathed in deeply.

After he had ended his last relationship, many years ago, he had lived a life alone up on the mountain, with only his dragon clan for company, and now, he was about to make a huge transition. After spending so much time by himself, he was about to head into the main part of Bridge Hollow, and help the bears and wolves guard the town while the supernatural convention was taking place. A yearly festival was arriving, within hours, that brought people from far and wide to their little mountain town, to explore all things paranormal, supernatural and mystical. But unlike in the past, now, it was cause for concern to everyone in the know.

Bridge Hollow was no longer safe. And Brax and the others were going to have to do their best to protect it.

He reached up and ran a big, rough hand through his black hair and sighed. After years of solitude, he dreaded the thought of being surrounded by so many people. Sure, he had gone into town on many occasions, but it would be completely different actually living there. To have to live and breathe the everyday happenings of a small town, and be recognized by all who saw him…

Continue the last tale in the Bridge Hollow series, here on Amazon…